OTHER BOOKS BY MONICA

SCOTTISH HISTORICAL:
Highland Untamed
Highlander Unmasked
Highland Unchained
Highland Warrior
Highland Outlaw
Highland Scoundrel
The Chief
The Hawk
The Ranger
The Viper
The Saint
The Recruit
The Hunter
The Knight (novella)
The Raider
The Arrow
The Striker
The Rock
The Rogue (novella)
The Ghost

REGENCY HISTORICAL:
The Unthinkable
Taming the Rake

CONTEMPORARY ROMANTIC
SUSPENSE:
Going Dark
Off the Grid
Out of Time

NYT & USA TODAY
BESTSELLING AUTHOR

MONICA McCARTY

HIGHLAND CROSSFIRE

A CAMPBELL TRILOGY NOVELLA

DEDICATION

To Sara Ramsey and Christie Ridgway who helped me finally (after almost ten years) put Annie and Niall's story together. We should always go to retreats at castles!

January 26, 2019

DEAR READER,

In the ten years since the Campbell trilogy was published, I've had many requests for Annie and Niall's story. I'd always intended to write it, but given the difficult subject matter of Annie's past, I wanted to make sure I did their story justice, and just what that story was hadn't really come to me. That changed a couple of years back when the first seedlings of a story began to take root. A writer's retreat at a fabulous "castle" in New York last summer gave me the time I needed to (finally!) put it all together.

To all the people who have written to me about Annie and Niall over the years, thank you for keeping them alive in my heart. It may have taken a little longer than planned, but this one is for you.

PROLOGUE

June 13, 1607, Dunvegan Castle, Isle of Skye

ANNIE MACGREGOR GLANCED AT THE man with the black expression on his face climbing the sea-gate stairs beside her and elbowed him in the ribs.

Hard.

"Ouch! Damn it, Annie," her brother said with a scowl. "What in Hades was that for?"

"You promised to have fun," she replied with a black scowl of her own. Patrick, the eldest of her three older brothers, wasn't the only one in the family with a temper. She resisted the urge to wag her finger at him. She wasn't going to be called a "London fishwife" (there was no worse disparagement to a Highlander than being called English) today. Today was going to be perfect. "You said that for one week we could have fun and not worry."

For one precious week they would emerge from their lair in the Lomond Hills and forget that they were outlaws, proscribed and persecuted simply for the sin of being MacGregors.

"I said I would *try* to have fun," Patrick corrected.

"And it's my job as chieftain to worry. Don't forget what happened last year." The prior year, Patrick, Gregor (her second eldest brother), and their cousin and chief, Alasdair MacGregor, had nearly been captured at the Highland Gathering held at Castle Campbell. Despite being outlawed, Alasdair, known as "the Arrow of Glen Lyon," had wanted to enter—and win—the archery contest. He would have, too, if Patrick hadn't betrayed their identities by coming to the aid of the Earl of Argyll's cousin Elizabeth who'd slipped in the mud. Annie's brother's actions had surprised them all. Patrick wasn't exactly known for his Galahad tendencies—especially toward the hated Campbells. "Besides," he added, probably knowing where her mind was heading and wanting to cut off questions about the incident, "little girls who use blackmail to get their way aren't in any position to be casting stones."

Annie's scowl shifted into a scrunched-up nose. "I didn't blackmail you. I cried."

"Exactly."

She bit back a smile as they passed through the first arched stone gate in the curtain wall. She'd been about five when she'd learned the destructive force of a woman's tears—especially hers—on her fearsome brothers. Although she rarely had to bring out that particular weapon to get her way, desperate times called for desperate measures, and Niall Lamont certainly qualified. She wasn't going to miss the chance to see him, and with the Gathering being held this year at Dunvegan Castle on the Isle of Skye—remote enough to be beyond the reach of the Campbells—she'd done what she had to do to convince her very unreasonable, overprotective, and extremely stubborn brother to let her attend.

If she didn't know better, she would think Niall was avoiding her. She hadn't seen him in almost six months—since he and his brother Malcolm had come to Glenstrae to fetch her brother Iain for their latest bit of mischief.

Niall and her brother Iain were always getting into mischief. It was what they did. They were young Highland warriors. Wild, wicked, and troublemaking was in the blood. When they weren't raiding and otherwise raising hell across the countryside, they were drinking and flirting with the sort of women she wasn't supposed to know about.

If the thought crossed her mind that there might be more than flirting going on, she turned her mind away from it. She wouldn't think about that. Whatever had happened before today was in the past.

Suddenly she thought of something else Patrick had said and elbowed him again even harder. As they'd reached the top of the stairs and were on the flat ground of the castle *barmkin*, she could stop to turn to face him, putting her hands on her waist and drawing herself up to her full height—even if it was a good foot shorter than his. "And I'm not a little girl. I'm eight and ten today."

He groaned and rubbed his side. "Don't remind me. My baby sister is all grown up, and I'm not sure how the hell that happened." He grimaced again with exaggerated pain. "You've gotten stronger in your old age."

She rolled her eyes as they continued on. "I've always been strong—just like you and Gregor." He started to open his mouth but, seeing her glare, slammed it shut. "Don't say it," she said, knowing exactly what he was thinking: "*Strong for a wee lass.*"

Strong was strong. Just because she wasn't as inhumanly strong as he was didn't mean she wasn't strong in her own right. She could carry more wood and move heavier stones than men much bigger than she.

But she wasn't supposed to notice things like that.

Nor would she point it out. She knew it upset her brothers that she had to work so hard. They were a proud, protective lot, and manual labor and rustic living conditions in whatever brae or glen they could find in the Lomond Hills that was safe from Campbells wasn't the life they wanted for her or thought she deserved. In another world, in another place where her clan hadn't had their lands and castles stolen from them, she would have lived the life of a noblewoman.

Once the MacGregors had ruled Scotland. Their motto, *s rìoghail mo dhream*, "royal is my race," attested to their ancient power. But over the years, the clan's authority had waned. And after the days of King Robert the Bruce, when the Campbells had started to rise in importance, the MacGregors had been slowly stripped of their wealth and had struggled to hold on to their lands.

That struggle had killed her parents. Her father had been a MacGregor chieftain—brother to the Chief of MacGregor—and her mother had been sister to Duncan Campbell of Glenorchy who was one of the most powerful men in Scotland. But her father and her Campbell uncle had fought over land, and when "Black" Duncan's men came to their castle on Loch Earn, her father had been killed in the attack.

Her mother had also been struck down that night by her own brother's men. Unintentionally, maybe, but caught in the crossfire nonetheless. A not-uncommon fate of women in the Highlands where war and feuds between the clans had gone unchecked by powerless kings for hundreds of years.

But the once-unfettered power of the clans and chiefs was waning. King James the VI of Scotland, and now the I of England, intended to put an end to the lawlessness in the Highlands, and this time it was the MacGregors who were caught in the crossfire. Outlawed and made a scapegrace for wrongs they didn't commit to appease the Scottish king's new English subjects.

But none of that mattered today. Today Annie was free. Today she was finally eighteen. Today she would see the man she'd given her heart as a woman full grown. There would be no more excuses. No more waiting. He would kiss her, and then he would ask her to marry him.

Niall Lamont might be a rogue, but he loved her. Of that she had no doubt.

Almost as if Patrick could read her mind, he frowned. There was a familiar warning in his voice when he started, "Annie…"

I don't want you to be disappointed.

But she wasn't listening. She'd just caught sight of the man striding out of the massive square tower ahead of her. The man she'd traveled so far to see. The man who made her breath hitch, her chest ache, and her stomach drop since the first time she'd seen him, even though she'd been but ten years old.

Eight years later, Niall Lamont, the second son of the Lamont of Ascog, was still one of the most handsome men she'd ever beheld. He had pitch-black hair, brilliant blue eyes, and a smile that would melt even the steeliest of knees. Nearly as tall as her towering brother at a few inches over six feet, his broad shoulders already supported an impressive bulk of lean muscle that in five years' time—when he was the same age as Patrick's six and twenty—might even surpass her brother's powerful warrior's physique.

But that was where the similarities between the two men ended. Patrick had had little reason to smile in the sixteen years since he'd witnessed their parents' deaths and been forced to take up the mantle of chieftain to a persecuted clan. But Niall on the other hand... Niall did nothing but smile. A wicked, cocksure smile that lit the blue in his eyes with a silvery twinkle and made her feel as if she'd just stepped out into the bright sunlight every time he looked at her.

Even that first time when she was ten and he'd come up behind her after she'd punched that horrid Torquil MacNeil in the nose for trying to kiss her.

"Now, that's the lass for me," Niall had said, breaking out into peals of laughter.

His words had seemed prophetic. They were perfect together. And in the dozens of times they'd met since then, she'd never had cause to doubt it. It was in the way he looked at her. The way the light jumped into his eyes. The way their gazes would catch and hold and something pure and powerful would pass between them. It happened every time.

Except this time.

This time when he looked at her the broad smile that had been on his face held for one long instant and fell. It slid from his eyes and took the twinkle—and the feel of sunlight—along with it in a hard crash of disappointment. He turned away so quickly to talk to the man beside him—his brother Malcolm, she realized—that the ground under her feet seemed to shift and roll. She felt unsteady. As if she were still standing on the planks of the *birlinn* she'd just gotten off of and bracing herself against the violent pitch of the sea.

His reaction was so unexpected—and so instantaneous—that she almost wondered whether he'd seen her.

But he had.

Annie's unfailing confidence where Niall Lamont was concerned dimmed. But not for long. Not when she noticed her brother's fearsome gaze in Niall's direction.

That was it! Her blasted brother was the reason for Niall's reaction. Annie knew the two men had had words last time she'd seen Niall. Patrick had discovered them in the barn together. They weren't doing anything, but he'd ordered her to leave and said something to Niall that had sent him running off with Iain with barely a goodbye.

She'd had to corner him to get that.

"I'm sorry, Annie. I can't do this. It isn't right."

She didn't understand what he was talking about. "What isn't right?"

He wouldn't look at her. He seemed pained somehow. "You're too young; you don't understand."

She'd gotten angry then. Those were her brother's words. "I'm seven and ten."

He smiled at that, and the sun came out again. "Practically an old woman." He laughed, but then quickly sobered. "People might get the wrong impression of us spending time together. They may think…" He seemed embarrassed. "They may think badly of you."

"Why? We aren't doing anything wrong." Much to her disappointment. "And you like *spending time with me."*

He didn't deny it. How could he? Niall loved her every bit as much as she loved him. Everyone knew it. He'd always made a point to seek her out. He talked to her in a way he didn't talk to anyone else. Told her things. Confided in her. Trusted her. There was an intimacy between them that went beyond friendship and compatibility.

"Then what's the problem?" she asked. "Why do you care what everyone thinks?"

She didn't care. The women who gossiped about her were just jealous.

He looked at her, shook his head, and laughed. "You're impossible to argue with."

"Good," she said with a lift of her chin. "Then don't. You can kiss me goodbye instead."

His face darkened ominously. Anyone who thought Niall only carefree and good-natured had never seen him get angry. He could turn terrifying in an instant. But all that male intimidation was lost on her. Niall would never hurt her. He would protect her with his life. "Annie… you have to stop saying that."

"Why?"

"Because you make it hard for me to do the right

thing."

"It isn't right to kiss me?"

He looked down at her, and the fierce expression on his face—the longing, the desire, the nearly palpable hunger—made her think he'd finally relent. That he'd finally give in to the attraction that had been building between them for years.

The air seemed to be sucked out of the space between them, and every inch of her skin was humming. She felt a crackle that sent sparks of heat racing through her blood as he leaned closer…

"No, damn it," he said, more to himself than to her, and jerked back. "Not when you are so young. You aren't even eighteen, for Christ's sake."

It took Annie a moment for her senses to clear from the almost kiss to manage a reply. "I won't be seventeen forever," she told him.

She could have sworn she heard him mumble "heaven help me" as he turned and walked away.

Well, heaven wasn't going to help him today. Today she would have her kiss—and the promise of the man she'd given her heart to many years before.

WHAT THE HELL WAS ANNIE DOING HERE? HER brother was half-crazed to risk taking her from the safety of the Lomond Hills. Although "safety" was a relative term when it came to the MacGregors. There wasn't anywhere that was truly safe for the hunted clan. But the wild, inhospitable countryside north of Loch Katrine that stretched to the Braes of Balquhidder was about as close as it came. There were few men brave enough to venture into the wolves' own den.

The Campbells and their leader, the Earl of Argyll, might not agree, but Alasdair MacGregor, the MacGregor of Glenstrae, didn't need a piece of paper to claim title to those lands. He held them by the right of sword and wouldn't relinquish them easily.

But if Niall were honest with himself, he'd admit that safety wasn't the only reason for the fierceness of his reaction—or the black mood that seemed to suddenly darken the sunny day. It was the feeling of being caught. Of knowing he couldn't hide. Of being forced to confront something that he would rather ignore.

What was between him and Annie… he wanted to keep it that way forever. He wanted to bottle it up and protect it from the stench of duty and responsibility.

But they weren't children anymore—as both her brother and his liked to remind him—and he could no longer pretend otherwise. It had become harder and harder to resist the temptation that being with her brought. He knew just how close to kissing her he'd come last time, and that would have been a disastrous mistake—in more ways than one.

Even if he wished this moment would never come, he knew it was here. And that was the real reason for Niall's anger.

Still, he couldn't completely ignore the spike of pleasure at seeing her. There had never been another woman who could make him feel the way that Annie did. It wasn't her beauty. Although he wasn't blind; he'd noticed that the adorable ten-year-old scamp with tangled hair and freckled cheeks who had leveled a boy half a head taller than her with a punch to the nose had grown into a young woman of exceptional beauty.

It was just that her looks had never been what had attracted him. It was the fierceness of her spirit, the brash stubbornness, the indelible pride, and the girlish mischievousness—not the stunning green of her eyes, the golden glow of her complexion, or the dark, whisky-colored locks that flowed down her back in a tumble of silk-smooth and very *un*tangled waves. Nor was it the strength of her long, slender limbs, the curve of her hips, or the lush roundness of her breasts—although those sure as hell had caused him a lot of pain and long, sleepless nights the past couple of years.

No, Annie was as wild and strong as the land that her clan fought so hard to hold on to. Whatever excess confidence and arrogance he might be accused of having, she met him step-by-step. She'd captivated him from the first moment he'd seen her, even though he'd only been a lad of fourteen.

There was no one like her.

But she wasn't for him.

He knew that. He just didn't want to have to think about it.

Niall didn't have any desire for a wife as yet—he was only one and twenty, for God's sake—but when he did marry, it was his duty to make it a good one. His marriage would be a political alliance brokered to better the clan. And the outlawed MacGregors—even if Iain MacGregor was one of his best friends and he respected the hell out of Patrick MacGregor—weren't a clan that anyone wanted to be connected with right now. Especially the Lamonts. The longtime bond between the two clans had already cast Campbell suspicion in the Lamont direction. A bond of marriage would only make that scrutiny worse.

Marrying a MacGregor wouldn't just be a failure of Niall's duty to his clan, it could also be dangerous.

His brother Malcolm, who like their father had pointed this out more than once, hadn't missed the exchange across the *barmkin*. "You have to tell her. It isn't fair to the lass."

"Tell her what? I've never made her any promises."

Niall knew he sounded like an arse—a defensive arse—which was appropriate since that's how he felt. But Malcolm's pitying look made it feel as if his skin was being peeled back and salt rubbed in it.

"Maybe not, but sometimes verbal promises aren't necessary. That lass has loved you for years. And despite your efforts to prove otherwise lately, I don't think you are as unattached as you want to be."

Niall's jaw clamped down. He didn't need his older brother lecturing him on having a little fun—Malcolm did his share of sowing his wild oats—and any attachment he might feel was irrelevant. People of their station didn't marry for "attachment."

"If it's any consolation," Malcolm said. "I wish it could be different."

Niall held his brother's gaze, and seeing nothing but compassion, could only nod. "Me, too."

The words hurt to admit. It felt as if they'd had

to be pried out from between his ribs with an iron crow.

The two men had crossed the yard to where the other contestants were gathered, so the conversation came to a happy end. But all too soon Niall was forced to remember it when Annie—looking exceptionally pretty in a colorful *arisaidh*—cornered him as he was walking back to the great hall from the archery practice area.

Before he could stop her, she grabbed his hand and dragged him into the castle herb garden. Unfortunately for him, it was located in a private corner of the *barmkin*, and there didn't seem to be anyone else around.

Like a coward, he'd looked.

Barely had she let his hand go, and he'd recovered his senses before she turned on him in a huff. "Whatever is the matter with you?"

"What do you mean?"

Playing dumb with Annie was never a good thing to do. Her eyes narrowed like those of a predator who had just smelled blood. The MacGregors were known as Sons of the Wolf, but right now he thought that should be sons *and* daughters.

"You acted like you didn't know me when you saw me this morning. Have I changed so much in *six* months that you didn't recognize me, or are you too busy impressing all the swooning lasses to deign to bestow a wave of hello to me?"

He didn't miss either jab: the reproaching for both his long absence and the meaningless smiles and winks he'd exchanged with the women who were watching his practice for the games.

"They don't mean anything to you," she added.

He didn't like the certainty in her voice. Had he been trying to prove a point to himself or to her by flirting a little more intently today?

"I didn't say they did. But it's no business of yours."

He should know better than to try to embarrass her. Annie didn't have a bone of maidenly modesty in her body. She knew who she was. She might be poor, hunted, and forced to live in the hills like a villein most of the time, but she was a MacGregor, and the proud lineage of her clan permeated every fiber of her being. No matter how low they tried to bring her, or whether she was gowned in fine silks or in a frayed and threadbare wool plaid, she was as regal as any queen.

As if to prove his point, his comment elicited nothing but the raising of one delicately arched eyebrow. "Isn't it?"

He wouldn't answer that. "What do you want, Annie? I need to change before the evening meal."

She looked puzzled by his impatience rather than hurt. She tilted her head, and a small half smile turned her pretty pink, bow-shaped mouth.

He felt an ache in a place that told him he *really* needed to stop thinking about the shape—and softness—of her mouth. Or how it would feel and taste crushed under his. Or how it would look wrapped around…

He cursed inwardly. But at one and twenty, this was the usual direction of his thoughts. Preoccupied was more like it. But he was a man and he needed to act like it.

"I guess you must have forgotten what day it is. I thought you might want to wish me something?"

Hell, he had forgotten! It was the Ides of June. "Damn it, Annie. I'm sorry. Happy Saint's Day."

She grinned and moved closer to stand before him. A little too close for his peace of mind, but he wouldn't make it awkward by taking a step back as he wanted.

She looked up at him expectantly. Her tilted doe eyes half-lidded and almost coy. "I think you've forgotten something else." At his confused look she gave him a hint. A *big* hint. She leaned in enough to let the firm tips of her breasts graze his chest. She might have dipped a torch to oil, so quickly did his blood light on fire. He would have wondered whether the unusually brazen move was a mistake were it not for her next huskily spoken words. "It's my *eighteenth* Saint's Day."

Niall felt the blood drain to his feet in a hard rush. Gazing down into that upturned face so close to his own, he felt something jam in his chest.

He knew exactly what she meant—what she was asking for. And if he had any doubt, the inviting parting of her lips took it all away.

For years he'd wanted to do nothing more than kiss her. He'd wanted to dip his head, cover those enticingly pink lips with his, and give in to the passion that flamed between them. He sensed how good—how hot—it would be.

Perhaps that was what gave him the strength to refuse the nearly irresistible temptation of her not-so-innocent invitation. The knowledge that once broached this road would be a much harder one not to go down in the future.

But when he tried to step back, he realized the wall of the kitchen was behind him. Then her arms were laced around his neck, her body was leaning into his, and all his good sense vanished with the gentle press of her mouth to his.

Ah hell.

The velvety softness and sweet honey taste stole his breath. For one perilous second, he felt paralyzed, poised on the precipice of indecision. Of something big. Of something he wasn't sure he was ready to handle.

But when she sighed, the decision was ripped from him in a responding groan of longing so deep he wasn't sure where it had come from. All he knew was that he had to have her. He had to kiss her. He had to feel her lips move under his and feel her body pressing into him.

God, how many times had he dreamed of this?

Niall wrapped her in his arms, pulled her against his chest, and gave in to the rush of desire that capsized his good intentions and sent him drowning in a whirlpool of pleasure so intense that he wasn't sure he would be able to pull himself out.

AT THE FIRST TOUCH OF HIS LIPS ON HERS, ANNIE knew the long wait and moments of uncertainty were worth it. This… *this* was what she'd always known was between them. This was why none of those other women whom he smiled at or flirted with mattered.

It was the overwhelming feeling of warmth, of security, and joy that came over her when Niall pulled her into his arms. It was the certainty of destiny fulfilled. The affirmation of fate long awaited.

They belonged together, and no one would ever be able to convince her differently. He might smile and flirt and tease, but he was hers. Niall Lamont had always been hers. Just as she was his.

When he groaned and deepened the kiss, when his mouth moved over hers possessively, when she felt him give in to the power and harness it with the smooth delicious strokes of a man intent on pleasure, she knew Niall understood it as well.

She loved the way he tasted like the split birch twigs he absently chewed on that were vaguely sweet and wintry. She loved the way he took control. She loved the way his strong arms held her and the granite hardness of his chest surrounding her.

Perhaps it was the long wait—the anticipation—that explained what happened next. That explained how a kiss could go from slow and exploratory to wild and out of control with a few tentative swipes of a tongue. A tongue that was in her mouth and sliding against hers, sparring, circling, sliding deeper and deeper into a chasm of pleasure.

She'd never felt anything like this. It was as if she'd fallen down a dark tunnel of need and passion, and nothing else mattered.

She'd touched him so many times, but it had never been like this. It had never felt so desperate and frantic. Muscles that her hands might have accidentally grazed before she now clutched as if they were a lifeline. He felt so wonderfully hard—and strong. She couldn't seem to press into the granite-hard shield of his chest deep enough. Close enough. Her breasts were crushed but achy and throbbing for more.

Innocently, she pressed her hips against his and felt…

Good gracious.

He cursed and pushed her away with enough force to send her stumbling back.

"We can't do this, damn it!" he bit out, his voice ragged and teeming with something she didn't understand.

Why was he so angry?

"Why not?" She reached for him as if it were the most natural thing in the world, but the unconscious gesture seemed to make him even angrier.

He pushed her hands away as if she were a leper. "Damn it, Annie, stop it! I can't marry you!"

The cold slap of his words jerked her head back. For a long moment, her heart didn't beat.

You must have heard him wrong.

But she hadn't. His words echoed loudly in her ears.

Stunned, she looked into the handsome face of the boy—the man—she thought she knew so well and felt a wave of confusion and hurt that was so strong it washed away all vestiges of what they'd just shared in one hard swoop. The body that had seconds before been hot and liquid now felt cold and bereft.

Wordlessly, her eyes raked his face, searching for… something. Anything that might explain what he meant.

But what she saw looked mostly like discomfort. As if he would rather be anywhere else in the world than here with her. Which hurt all the more because she felt exactly the opposite.

When the shock wore off enough, she finally

managed, "Why not?"

He dragged his fingers through the wavy, jaw-length dark hair that had a tendency to fall across one side of his face. "God, Annie, how can you ask that?" He sounded pained. As if her question were torturing him. "Don't you see?"

Her eyes locked on his. She could tell from the heat in his cheeks that he wanted to turn away.

He was embarrassed. Why would he be embarrassed?

Suddenly she sucked in her breath, the pain slicing through her lungs and heart like a razor-sharp dirk. She did see. Her brother had been right. Patrick had warned her many times, but she'd never listened because she'd been so sure that she and Niall were different.

But Niall was saying that he couldn't marry her because she was a MacGregor.

Because he thought she wasn't good enough for him.

Annie was far from oblivious to the realities of the world they lived in. She knew better than anyone how much the MacGregor fortunes had fallen—she lived it every day. She knew that some considered them nothing more than cutthroats and outlaws. She knew that she had little to offer him besides herself.

She'd just foolishly—naïvely—thought that she would be enough.

Annie had been poor and without a home for most of her life. She'd spent more time living in hovels than in castles. She'd only been two when her parents had been killed. Dispossessed of their home and any wealth they might have had, the four orphaned children had been forced to rely on the generosity of relatives for years.

Annie knew what it was like to feel as if you were taking food from the mouth of a starving child because she'd been in that horrible position. She knew what it was like to be poor and unwanted. To be stripped of everything you had and try to find a way to survive.

But never had she been made to feel ashamed about it. Never had she been made to feel unworthy by someone she cared about.

Until now.

That it was from the person she loved the most in the world made it all the more painful.

Niall was every inch the untamed Highland warrior and might not have any more courtly graces than she did, but his father, the Lamont of Ascog, was a powerful chief. Annie was...

For one horrible moment she saw herself as he must see her, and she wanted to crawl into a hole and die of shame.

But only for a moment.

She stepped back. Her gaze hardening. Pride, the one thing no one could take from her, wrapping around her heart like an iron shield. "I do see now," she said, her voice as icy as the winter winds on the top of Ben Nevis. She looked him straight in the eye. "You don't think I'm good enough for you."

He winced, a pained expression on his face like a man who'd been forced to swallow something that tasted rotten. "Jesus, Annie, it's not like that."

Her spine stiffened even more, her chin lifting even higher. "It's not? Of course it is. At least be man enough to admit it."

He frowned. No man—especially a young Highland warrior—appreciated a slur on his manhood. But manhood was far more than prowess on the battlefield—or prowess between the bedsheets. It was taking responsibility for your actions even when you might not want to. It was about standing up for what was right even when that might not be easy. It was admitting what you were doing, no matter how unpleasant or harsh.

How many times had her brother tried to warn her that the seemingly wild rogue was an ambitious man? And how many times had she refused to hear him? Refused to consider that Niall would see her as anything other than a prize no matter what the size of her tocher.

Annie had expected too much from Niall Lamont. She could see that now. She'd expected him to see beyond the difficulty, beyond the size of her purse, beyond the king's persecution. She'd expected him to see that no matter how low the MacGregors had been brought by circumstances, she was still a woman he should be proud to take as his wife. She'd expected him to put his heart above his duty and ambition. But most of all, she'd expected him to love her as much as she loved him.

Maybe it had been unrealistic, but it didn't stop her from hating him for making her feel this way.

"Damn it, don't be like this," he said with a pleading note she'd never heard in his voice before. "You know how I feel about you."

She shook her head and looked him straight in the eye. "No. No, I don't think I do. I believe I was quite mistaken."

She wasn't making it easy on him, and her cold

stoicism in the face of his distress was clearly making him angry. "I'm not ready to get married."

"That is obvious."

His eyes narrowed, hearing the slur. "Don't you see? I have a responsibility! A duty! Even if I wanted to marry you, my father would never allow it."

"Even if I wanted…" Despite the steel around her heart, that unthinking dart still penetrated.

She should just walk away. But she couldn't stop herself from asking, "And what about that kiss? Did that mean nothing to you?"

Another wince and another uncomfortable drag of his hand through his hair. "Christ, Annie. What do you want me to say? It was just a kiss."

She held his gaze for a moment, silently challenging that assessment. But he was the one with experience. He was the one who would know.

Still, somehow, she knew he was lying. "So, it was nothing special? It meant nothing to you?"

His mouth clamped in an angry line. "What the hell do you want me to say?"

I love you, and there is no woman I would be prouder to have by my side as my wife. Will you make me the happiest man in the world and marry me?

The words she'd hoped to hear taunted her with her own stupidity. Her own simplicity.

She looked at him. She would not grovel. She would not beg. She would not show him how much he'd hurt her today. How he'd crushed her hopes and dreams for the future with his duty and responsibility. And worse, how he'd made her feel every bit as low as the king and Campbells had tried to bring them.

"I don't want you to say anything." She meant it.

"Goodbye, Niall."

And before he could say another word, Annie MacGregor walked away. Her pride intact but everything else shattered.

CHAPTER ONE

❧

Edinample Castle, Loch Earn, August 1609

ANNIE KNELT ON THE TURF bank of the rectangular vegetable garden, clearing weeds from the neatly planted rows of onions, beets, and peas. A sharp gust of wind tore a wisp of long, dark hair from its pins. She struggled to catch the errant lock for a minute before tucking it once more behind her ear.

With the wind, she felt a prickle of awareness race along her skin—the familiar sensation of being watched—that cast a black shadow over the otherwise sunny day.

He was back.

She clenched her mouth in a tight, angry line, ignoring the sensation—as well as the man who'd provoked it—and went on tending the garden.

A few minutes later, another man's voice broke through the silence of her thoughts. "Ah, here you are. I wondered where you'd disappeared to."

Annie could hear the worry in her brother's voice and tried not to let it anger her. She was in the garden, for goodness' sake. Surrounded by five-foot-thick stone walls and the dozens of guardsmen who patrolled them. No one could hurt her here.

But reminding herself that Patrick's distress came from a place of love and helplessness, she tried to control her frustration. "I'm fine, and as you can see, perfectly safe. You need to stop worrying about me. I'm not a glass poppet about to shatter; I'm tougher than I look."

She wouldn't let what had happened destroy her, even if at times she wondered if it was already too late. She didn't know who she was anymore. Or what she wanted. For so many years she'd thought Niall was the measure of her future happiness. But that simple, lovestruck girl whose thoughts centered on a husband and children no longer existed. She didn't know who had replaced her, just that she was gone.

Her eyes met her brother's, and the sadness in his gaze made her chest pinch. She knew he was trying to help the only way he knew how, but didn't he realize that his protectiveness and well-meaning smothering was making it worse? It was making her unable to forget.

If it were possible to forget.

It *had* to be possible. That was the only thing keeping her going. And day by day, little by little, it *was* getting better.

"I know that, and I'm sorry. I just can't seem to help it. Lizzie said I'm going to drive you both crazy with my 'cosseting.'" He cursed with disgust. "I don't know what the hell has happened to me. I've gone completely crazed with irrational fears since the baby was born. Do you know I moved the cradle away from the window last night in case a tree blew over in the wind and broke through the glass?"

"You mean the freshly cut-down tree that I had to climb over to get to the garden?"

He muttered a long stream of curses and she laughed, surprised at how good it felt. Of late there had been precious little to laugh about for all of them.

Annie thought the worst thing that could happen to her was having the man she loved break her heart. But the past two years had proved her wrong.

Very wrong.

First had come the disastrous battle between the MacGregors and Colquhouns at Glenfruin where four hundred of her clansmen had lost their lives. But if having her clan decimated in battle wasn't bad enough, what had come after was infinitely worse. Thanks to some theatrics by the Colquhoun widows, including parading blood-soaked sarks before the notoriously squeamish king, the persecution of the MacGregors and efforts to bring them to "justice" had intensified and taken a vicious turn.

Justice, this time, included the heads of her clansmen. Bounties were given to the bearer of MacGregor heads, entitling the person to their holdings. But it wasn't just the MacGregors being hunted. It was also their allies. The punishment for harboring the outlawed clan was death and the forfeiture of lands.

There had been nowhere for them to hide.

They'd seen that firsthand when her cousin Alasdair's men, including her brothers, had called upon an ancient bond of hospitality between the Mac-

Gregors and Lamonts to take refuge on the Isle of Bute last summer. Colin Campbell, the Campbell of Auchinbreck at the time, had hunted them down and attacked the Lamont's Ascog Castle, burning it practically to the ground.

Niall's father, the Chief of Lamont of Ascog, and his older brother, Malcolm, had both been killed along with forty of their clansmen. Niall and his young brother, Brian, were also thought lost, but they'd managed to escape to Ireland. They'd returned to Scotland a few months later on hearing that Alasdair MacGregor was surrendering after agreeing to the Earl of Argyll's promise to escort him to England to put his case before King James.

Niall's sister, Caitrina, had married Jamie Campbell, Colin's younger brother and one of the most feared men in the Highlands, to seal the bargain. But both Alasdair MacGregor and apparently Jamie Campbell had been tricked by the wily Earl of Argyll, known as "Archibald the Grim." Alasdair was indeed escorted to England. But as soon as the MacGregor chief stepped down on English soil—technically satisfying the terms of Argyll's "promise"—he was immediately brought back to Scotland and executed along with eleven of his remaining chieftains and guardsmen, including Annie's brother Iain.

Annie's heart squeezed. The brother who caused so much mischief with Niall now had his head on a pike alongside their cousin's and uncle's atop the gate of Holyrood Palace.

Retribution for Argyll's trick, or "Highland Promise," as the dastardly deed had become known, had been swift, with the remaining MacGregor clansmen and allies calling for Fire and Sword. The risings that followed had gone on for months and stretched across the Highlands from Rannoch Mor to Glenorchy.

In his rage and bloodlust, her brother Gregor had committed an unforgivable act. He'd ordered the rape of a Campbell woman whom they'd come across in one of their raids. Gregor's offenses did not end there. He'd attempted to kill Elizabeth Campbell and challenged Patrick's position as chief after the death of their cousin. Gregor had paid for those sins when he was captured by Jamie Campbell last winter and executed.

She'd lost two brothers in almost as many months.

But she could not mourn Gregor as she did Iain and her other kinsmen. Not after what Gregor had done. Even if she understood where the blackness that had curdled his soul came from. The MacGregors had been treated like dogs for so long, it was hardly a surprise that one had turned rabid.

No, Annie's inability to forgive her brother came from another, far more personal, place. She did not blame him for what happened to her, but she could not forgive him for doing to another woman what had been done to her either.

Annie had been caught in the crossfire of Gregor's misdeeds. In retribution for the rape of the Campbell woman, the Laird of Auchinbreck, Colin Campbell, had ordered the rape of a MacGregor "whore" and fifty merks to the person who could bring him a kinswoman of Gregor MacGregor.

She'd been that kinswoman. Annie had been the woman raped when her hiding place in the Braes of Balquhidder had been betrayed by a local farmer whose lands—and crops—had been accidentally burned by Gregor's men.

Three of Colin Campbell's soldiers had brutalized her. Ripped her clothes from her body, lowered their vile, repulsive bodies on top of her, and violated her. It might have gone on until her death if some of her clansmen hadn't arrived and mounted enough of a battle to get her away.

Rape was an all-too-common occurrence in feuds and wars between the clans, where men thought it a way to shame their enemy. But knowing that it was part of the time they lived in didn't make it any easier to bear.

Battered, bruised, and brutalized, Annie had taken refuge on the Isle of Molach in Loch Katrine to recover. That had been ten months ago. Her body had healed, the cuts and bruises long faded. But the memories were far harder to erase. For months she'd woken up screaming in a cold sweat, the faces of her tormentors swimming in front of her in the darkness of her dreams. She could hear their hateful grunts and taunts. Feel their blows against her face and body as she tried to fight back. But the nightmares had lessened, and slowly life was drawing her back in.

She didn't flinch when someone accidentally touched her anymore.

Her month-old new nephew, Iain—named for the brother killed along with their beloved former chief—was perhaps part of that. His birth had been like a ray of sunshine for them all. His sweet innocence was a much-needed reminder that not everything was dark and ugly in this world.

"I know exactly what happened to you," Annie

said to her brother. "You fell in love. And now you have a baby to love as well."

Patrick smiled, something that had been so rare before, but since Lizzie had come into his life was much more frequent.

With all that had happened, it was hard to believe that a Campbell and MacGregor could find love. But her brother and sister-in-law gave proof that miracles did happen. Patrick MacGregor, chief of an outlawed clan, had fallen in love with Elizabeth Campbell, the favored cousin of the Earl of Argyll and sister to Duncan Campbell, the new Laird of Auchinbreck, and Jamie Campbell. She was also sister to the man responsible for Annie's rape.

But Annie knew better than anyone else not to attribute the sins of the brother to the sister. Lizzie was no more responsible for Colin than Annie was for Gregor. But it was still strange to think that much of their recent good fortune was because of a Campbell. Duncan, Jamie, and Elizabeth had forced their powerful cousin, the Earl of Argyll, to make amends for his perfidy by restoring Patrick to his lands and looking the other way when "justice" was meted out to Colin Campbell.

Still, the enmity and hatred between the Campbells and the MacGregors had gone on for so long it was hard to think of them any other way.

But she would try. For her brother's sake as much as her own. She'd meant what she said to him. She was tougher than she looked. Colin Campbell's men had hurt her—changed her, maybe—but she would not let them destroy her.

Annie didn't realize she'd resumed weeding until Patrick said, "You don't have to do that anymore, you know."

Aye, the MacGregors (or "Murrays," as they were forced to call themselves—the name MacGregor was still proscribed) had indeed come up in the world with Patrick's marriage. They not only had the family lands back, they also had a castle full of servants.

"I know," she said with a wry smile. "But I like it. I'm used to being busy."

It was being a lady that she wasn't used to. Since she'd come to Edinample last month to help with the birth of the baby, her new sister-in-law's generosity had been overwhelming—and embarrassing. For the first time in her memory, Annie had new gowns—lowland gowns made of fine silks and wools—more slippers than she could wear in a lifetime, shawls, a wool hauberk, and a matching set of pearl earrings and necklace. Patrick had warned her that the diminutive and waifish Lizzie could be stubborn, but Annie hadn't believed it until she'd tried to refuse some of her sister-in-law's "gifts."

Suddenly her brother's attention was drawn to the hillside opposite the castle. He must have sensed what Annie had earlier. The return of her unwanted sentinel.

"Will you see him this time?"

Annie stiffened reflexively, her spine as straight as an arrow protruding from its quiver. "No. Nothing has changed."

Patrick's raised brows told her he was about to challenge that assessment. "He killed Colin Campbell, made himself an outlaw in doing so, and gave up his right to be Chief of Lamont for you. I'd say quite a bit has changed."

Yes, now Niall Lamont had been brought as low as he'd thought her.

Annie felt the familiar fury bubbling inside her. "I didn't ask him to do any of that—nor did I want him to. It wasn't Niall's place to kill Colin Campbell."

It was hers. The way she saw it, Niall Lamont had robbed her of her vengeance.

As if he could read her mind, her brother's gaze narrowed with concern. He didn't understand her need for vengeance. Her anger. What was viewed as a natural instinct for a man was seen as unnaturally "bloodthirsty" in a woman. Patrick didn't question his own thirst for vengeance against Colin Campbell—Niall had saved Patrick from having to kill his wife's brother—but hers made him uncomfortable.

But right now he just looked disgusted with himself. "I knew I should never have told you that story. I'm sure none of it is true."

Her mouth curved. She believed every word of the family legend. One of her MacGregor ancestors had reputedly married the illegitimate daughter of Robert the Bruce, who herself had trained to be a warrior and was said to have saved the life of the warrior king.

"Whether it's true or not makes no difference."

"You haven't given up your plan then?" It was more of a sad statement than a real question.

She quirked an eyebrow. "Because you refused to teach me? No. I haven't. Someone else has agreed to help."

He frowned, guessing to whom she referred. "Have a care with the lad, Annie. Robbie has worshipped the ground you walk on since he was a boy."

She better than anyone knew the heartbreak of unrequited love, and her brother's admonishment gave her a flicker of unease. Robbie knew she did not return his feelings. She'd told him many times as kindly as she could. But she could not deny that she might have taken advantage of his feelings for her in asking him to help her.

"Then you train me," she said.

He made a sharp sound that said, "not a chance." "You know how I feel about this. I won't forbid it, but I sure as hell won't encourage it. Next thing you know my wife will be outside alongside you trying to swing a sword."

If she'd been through what I went through, you might want her to know how to defend herself.

Annie wanted to say it, but she didn't. She knew how hard it was for her big, strong brother to be reminded that he hadn't been able to protect her. But no one could protect someone else all the time—no matter how big and strong they were. That was the point. That was why she wanted to do this. The only person who could protect her was her, and Annie intended to take control of her own defenses.

She'd fought back with a ferocity that had surprised her attackers. It had taken three of them to pin her down. But even though she was extremely strong for her size and sex, they'd eventually been able to overpower her. She'd been able to get in some damage but not enough.

If she'd known how to use a knife, it might have been different. Maybe she would have been able to give herself time to escape. Maybe she wouldn't have felt so helpless. Maybe she could have killed one of the scourges to prevent him from doing it to someone else.

"I think all women should know how to defend themselves."

Annie didn't realize she'd said it out loud until she saw the sadness—and guilt—on her brother's face.

It was a man's job to protect his women. That was what Patrick thought. That is what *the entire world* thought. By doing this, not only was she upsetting the natural order of things, it was also making it seem as if she didn't have faith in him. Patrick saw her wanting to learn how to fight as his failure. He didn't understand that it had nothing to do with him. This was about her.

But maybe she didn't give her big brother enough credit. When he voiced the reason for his concern, it didn't have anything to do with his ability to keep her safe. "Training with weapons is dangerous, Annie. I just don't want to see you get hurt."

That was something they could both agree on. "Neither do I. That's why I need to do this."

Their eyes held, and he nodded. "I'll tell Robbie you can start tomorrow."

She smiled broadly, for the first time in a long time feeling like herself. "Thank you, Patrick. You won't regret this."

He laughed. "I already do. A lass training to be a warrior? What will you be wanting next?"

She eyed him playfully. "Those trews you are wearing look comfortable. How about some of those?"

He rolled his eyes and guffawed. "Lasses wearing trews? I'd like to see that. Maybe you'd like wings to fly to the moon, too?"

One Week Later

"I'M SORRY, NIALL. THERE IS NOTHING I CAN DO. You know how stubborn Annie can be. She doesn't want to see you."

Niall's jaw clenched. He could see the sympathy in Patrick MacGregor's expression—sympathy that hadn't been there before the other man's marriage. But it seemed that the new MacGregor chief had learned that when it came to lasses and matters of the heart, sometimes you made mistakes. *Big* mistakes. Mistakes that Patrick, at least, had had forgiven.

If Niall could just go back to that day at Dunvegan…

It hadn't taken him long to realize that he'd made a mistake. Part of him had known it when Annie walked away. The sick feeling twisting his gut had been trying to tell him. But he'd mistaken it for guilt.

He hadn't meant to hurt her. Hadn't meant her to think that she wasn't good enough for him. He'd been one and twenty and trying to act like a man and do his duty, damn it. She should have understood that.

But what he'd attributed to guilt had quickly turned to anger. Her cold attitude and refusal to look at him the rest of the week had infuriated him. She'd acted as if she didn't care when the women had swarmed him after he'd won the foot race. When he'd overheard her say that it was no surprise as "Lamonts were good at running away," he'd nearly made a fool of himself by storming across the hall and forcing her to take back her words.

Instead he'd let one of the prettier lasses fawn all over him. But that had been a mistake as well. The woman's compliments and admiration only made him feel more pathetic for seeking it out, and nothing the lass said could make up for the disdain of the only woman who mattered.

But he'd been too damned proud to admit he'd made a mistake. He'd waited, trying to prove to himself over the next months that he was too young to want a wife. That it didn't matter whom he married. That kissing her wasn't special.

That he would be fine without her.

But by the time the Gathering had come to Ascog the following year, he'd realized what his body had been trying to tell him that day at Dunvegan. The illness that had gripped him wasn't guilt. It was panic. It was the knowledge that he'd done something horribly wrong that he might not be able to take back. That in trying to do his duty, he'd unintentionally made the woman he loved think she wasn't good enough. That to a proud woman like Annie that would be unforgivable.

When the MacGregors had called on the old bond of hospitality between the clans to take refuge near Ascog Castle, Niall had confided his mistake—and that he intended to make it right—to Iain. His friend had looked at him coldly and said, "She'll not have you now, and I can't say I blame her. You didn't want her."

Niall never had a chance to try to prove Iain wrong. Before he could attempt to make amends, Ascog was attacked, his father and brother killed, the MacGregor chief was tricked into surrendering and executed, Iain was killed, and Annie was…

He couldn't bear to think about it.

When Niall learned what had happened to her, he nearly went mad with rage and grief. He felt as if someone had taken a blade to him and sliced him right across the middle. Eviscerated him. Pulled out his insides and burned them right in front of his eyes.

He'd known then the full horror of his mistake and the cost of his stupidity. If he'd swallowed his pride earlier, he could have protected her. He could have prevented it from happening.

He refused to listen to anyone telling him differently.

He'd gone to her, ready to beg her forgiveness, ready to crawl on his hands and knees if he had to, to do whatever he could to prove to her how much he loved her.

But she refused to see him. Through the window that day, he could hear her tell her brother that she never wanted to see him. To send him away. That he was dead to her.

She was bruised and bloody—beaten to within an inch of her life—and hearing those words come out of her mouth when all he wanted to do was hold her in his arms had been a blow that he still had not recovered from.

He'd wanted to push his way in there and make

her listen to him, but her brothers had held him back and told him that it would be a mistake. That he needed to give her time. That he needed to be patient.

Niall knew exactly how to bide his time. He'd gone after Colin Campbell with a vengeance that only had one possible end. The man who'd ordered Annie raped had died at the end of Niall's sword in a forest on the road to Inveraray last winter.

Despite the efforts on Niall's behalf by his new Campbell brothers-in-law—Jamie and Duncan, the new Laird of Auchinbreck—Niall had been outlawed for it.

Ironically, his and Annie's positions had been reversed. But he wouldn't have it any other way. Niall had made his choice. He knew what he was doing and what he was giving up. And nothing would have prevented him from seeing justice done. *Highland* justice.

Colin Campbell had paid for his sins, but it seemed that Niall was still paying for his.

Niall's temper—which he'd been trying to restrain—flared. "I've been patient for months. How long is she going to punish me for this? Can't you do something?"

Patrick's gaze turned decidedly less friendly. "What would you have me do? Force her to see you?"

Niall paled, suddenly realizing how he sounded. "Jesus. Christ. No, of course not. I'm sorry. I'm just"—his furious pacing around the solar ended with him flopping down hard on a chair—"frustrated, damn it."

"Well, you'll have to be frustrated a little longer."

Patrick paused, seeming to debate with himself about whether to say more. "Annie has changed, Niall. She isn't the same girl you knew. You have to consider the possibility that she might never change her mind."

Niall thought about that practically every minute of every waking hour. And most of his sleep as well. It was what woke him up at night in a cold panic.

She has to forgive me.

He shook his head and told her brother what he told himself. "I can't let myself believe that. I have to have faith."

He'd failed her once, but he would not fail her again. He would keep coming back until she agreed to see him.

Annie had hoped that he'd given up. But a week after Niall made his first appeal to Patrick, she saw him riding through the gate again and made sure to avoid her brother's solar for the rest of the morning.

Which wasn't a problem as every morning before the midday meal for the past two weeks she and Robbie had been meeting in a secluded corner of the *barmkin* for him to instruct her in warfare. Or at least in skills that might help her defend herself, such as using a knife and, if she could get her instructor over his embarrassment, in hand-to-hand combat.

Her brother had come to watch a few times, but otherwise they'd been left alone. Annie was pretty

sure Patrick had told Robbie to use this corner
of the yard to be as far away from the other men
practicing as possible. He didn't want her to be a
distraction—or the cause of gossip.

He was too late for that, but she would not add
to his worry for her by pointing out the whispers
and pitying glances that followed her wherever she
went.

It seemed as if some people blamed her for
what had happened to her while others probably
thought she should have killed herself in shame.

But that sin had never crossed her mind. Even
in the confused haze and chaos of the hours and
days after she'd been brutalized, Annie had never
been confused about who the shame belonged to.
The vile men who'd raped her showed their own
weakness by doing what they'd done.

Her brother's expression was inscrutable the few
times he'd watched Robbie and her. But maybe
the gruffly issued corrections he'd given about
how she was standing or holding the practice knife
were praise enough. And perhaps even more tell-
ingly, he hadn't put a stop to it.

She didn't dare ask him about the trews though.
Although she'd meant it as a joke when she'd said
it, it quickly became apparent that the heavy folds
of her new gowns were going to get in her way.

After her foot caught on the hem for about the
tenth time, she had taken to practicing in a short
leine that fell to just above her knees and a bor-
rowed cotun to protect her chest and arms from
any accidental slices of the blade—theoretical slices
as she'd yet to touch a real blade. Her feet were
much too small for any of the men's boots, so she

wore simple soft leather brogues over her hose.

Once she was more proficient, she would wear her normal clothes. But while she was learning, the "peasant's garb," as Robbie had said when he first saw her in the simple linen tunic, would have to do.

Robbie... Annie sighed. The situation with her reluctant instructor was proving more complicated than she'd anticipated. It wasn't just that she feared Patrick was right—that the young warrior would grow increasingly attached from the time they were spending together—it was also that his discomfort with touching her or getting too close to her was impeding her ability to learn.

When she asked him to show her how to get out of a situation where someone comes up from behind her and grabs her, he'd lost so much color in his face she thought he was going to faint.

How was she supposed to learn to defend herself properly if they were always at arm's length?

By all rights, she should be the one discomforted by touch or closeness, but Robbie had always been like a brother to her. She could never see him as a threat to her.

In all other respects, however, Robbie was an excellent instructor, if perhaps a little overly cautious. He'd obviously taken her brother's words about safety to heart. Not only had she yet to see a steel blade, but he'd spent the better part of a week showing her how to properly draw the wooden practice knife from the leather sheath and belt he'd fashioned for her leg that also served as a garter for her woolen hose.

The double-edged *sgian-achlais*, which literally

translated to armpit knife, worn by Scottish warriors under their coat would be impractical for women's clothing, so Robbie had to devise something that would be hidden and yet accessible.

She'd been disappointed to not be learning how to wield the longer-bladed dirk, but Robbie assured her that she would be able to do plenty of damage with the five-inch blade of the *sgian-achlais*, and it would be much easier for her to handle.

In fact, they'd spent the next two days working on her handling of the small dirk. He'd shown her the different ways she could grip the handle in different situations until she felt comfortable.

Finally, the past couple of days, he'd shown her different slashing and thrusting techniques as he came toward threateningly.

Even with a wooden knife, it was harder than she'd thought it would be. She didn't want to accidentally hurt him. But after he chastised her for hesitating and holding back, she'd increased her efforts, and when she surprised him with a feigning slash followed by a sharp stab toward his stomach, she smiled with glee at his "ouch."

Her next attempt to trick him, however, didn't go as well. When Robbie came toward her this time, rather than direct her attack at his torso, she aimed for the deadly place on his upper thigh that he'd told her was a good target as it would kill a man quickly. He blocked her blow, but in her attempt to twist away, her foot tangled with his, and they both ended up on the ground. She flat on her back and Robbie—unfortunately—on top of her.

She didn't know who was more stunned or horrified by the hard slam of contact. Eyes wide, they stared at each other in silence for a moment until Annie felt the familiar panic crawling up her throat. She tried to tell herself that it was Robbie—her friend—but the press of weight and muscle weren't of a boy but that of a man.

And then she felt the proof of that manhood.

Something inside her snapped. All she could think of was getting him off her. She went half-crazed, screaming and trying to push him off, while Robbie, obviously shocked by her reaction, tried his best to leap backward off her and calm her down with stumbling apologies.

Annie's panic cleared as soon as his weight was off her. She blanched with shame and tried to think of something to say that would make the situation less embarrassing and awkward when things took a turn for the worse.

Suddenly Robbie—who was well over six feet tall and must be close to fourteen stone—was lifted off the ground by the scruff of his neck like a pup and slammed against the wall of the barn.

The slam shook the entire building—and the ground she was still sitting on.

A voice that was at once familiar but also changed reverberated through the air. "Give me one good reason why I shouldn't snap your foul neck."

Niall, Annie realized. A darker, gruffer, more deadly sounding Niall, but still the man she'd never wanted to see again.

CHAPTER TWO

𝒢

EMBARRASSMENT FORGOTTEN, ANNIE JUMPED TO her feet, her mouth pressed in a tight, furious line. She knew at once what Niall thought. Ignoring the fact that the same thought had caused her to panic a few moments ago, she hurled herself against Niall—or more specifically, Niall's far-thicker-with-muscle arm than she remembered that was pinning a red-faced, choking Robbie to the wall.

"Let go of him!"

How dare he try to play the gallant knight riding in to the rescue! It was too late for either. Niall Lamont had lost any claim to gallantry or rescuer on that horrible day over two years ago at Dunvegan.

Annie tugged and dragged at his leather-clad arm, pretty much putting her whole weight on it, but it didn't budge an inch. Good gracious, what did he do, eat steel all day?

"He can't breathe." She turned her head to look at the man she used to love, their eyes meeting for the first time. The hard thud in her chest and jolt that went along with it only angered her more.

There was nothing between them anymore. Nothing. No matter how piercing his blue-eyed gaze or how changed his appearance. His arm wasn't the only thing that had turned hard and steely. He looked every bit as brutal and dangerous as the outlaw he'd become.

What kind of fool woman found that attractive? She must have lost her mind. "Blast it, Niall, let go of him. Robbie didn't do anything."

Niall's expression showed no reaction to her plea. If anything, his gaze only grew more intense. Deadlier. "He was on top of you. I saw you trying to push him off."

Annie's cheeks flamed. From anger or shame, she didn't know which—maybe both. "It wasn't how it looked. We were training and I tripped. Robbie landed on top of me by accident, and I…" Her voice dropped off. She looked up at him to see Niall watching her intently, his expression still unreadable. But glancing sideways, she could see that he'd released his hold on Robbie enough for her friend to stop making those horrible sounds and for his color to return to normal. But as Niall still looked undecided about whether to let the other man go, she lifted her chin and added, "I forgot who he was for a moment, all right?"

She knew that Niall understood when he finally let Robbie go. But the sympathy in his gaze only increased her embarrassment and thus her anger.

She was furious not only that she'd lost control and panicked, but that Niall Lamont had stood witness to the moment of weakness. It was bad enough that Robbie had seen it.

She was done having people feel sorry for her.

Done feeling vulnerable. The Campbell soldiers had broken her, but she had every intention of putting herself back together. She couldn't do that, however, if everyone kept looking at her as if she were a fragile piece of glass that could shatter with one wrong touch.

She turned stiffly to Robbie and said matter-of-factly, "I'm sorry. I forgot where I was for a minute. It won't happen again." Before he could respond, she turned to Niall. "I can see why you jumped to the wrong conclusion, but your interference wasn't necessary. Whatever business you have with my brother, finish it and be on your way. You don't belong here, Niall."

Niall couldn't believe the change in Annie. The last time he'd seen her she'd been bruised and battered, as delicate and fragile as a broken bird. He'd been gutted—absolutely ripped apart—when she'd flinched from his gaze through that window.

But there was nothing delicate and fragile about her now—especially her tone, which had a distinctly imperious edge to it. *Royal is my race*, that was for sure. As happy as he was to see her healed and strong again, he admitted that he could have done without the haughty, indifferent attitude. Annie had never been indifferent to him. Never.

This had gone on long enough. Niall knew he'd hurt her terribly, but her stubbornness wasn't helping matters any. How were they going to get past this if she wouldn't deign to hear his apology?

"This is exactly where I belong," he said. "You're

here."

She made a sharp sound of protest, but before she could respond, he turned to the lad, whom he now recognized as one of Patrick MacGregor's clansmen. The boy's color and breathing had returned to normal, but he was still holding his throat where the pressure of Niall's grip was visible in blotches of red.

"Sorry about that, lad. But from where I was standing, it looked as if you were hurting her."

The young man's eyes narrowed, but it was clear that it wasn't Niall's apology that he objected to; it was the use of the word lad.

"Robert Mac—Murray. We met a few years back at the Games at Dunvegan before you were outlawed. I was a guardsman then, but I'm the chief's *Am Marischal Tighe* now."

Niall swore inwardly when Robbie unknowingly mentioned Dunvegan, where Niall had made such a horrible mess of everything. But when Annie's gaze hardened, Niall wondered whether the "lad" had done it intentionally.

Niall's own gaze narrowed as everything started to come back to him. He remembered Robbie now. He was the lad who'd looked longingly at Annie like a lovesick pup.

Robbie had changed. Although still young— probably a couple of years Niall's junior—he had added a few inches in height and a couple of stone in muscle.

Niall also knew that the mention of Robbie's place as seneschal in Patrick's guard hadn't been an accident. The lad was obviously an accomplished warrior to have achieved such an important position at his age.

But other things hadn't changed. If Robbie's embarrassment was any indication, his feelings for Annie were exactly the same.

"You caught me unaware," Robbie added, as if to explain how a warrior of his skill had been so overpowered.

Niall didn't think the result would have been any different if Robbie had seen him coming, but cognizant of a young man's pride, he let it go.

Suddenly the scene he'd stumbled onto came back to him. As did Annie's unusual clothes. He scanned her up and down, taking in the *leine*, hose, and too-big cotun. It almost looked as if she was... No. That was impossible.

Niall frowned. "What were you doing out here anyway?" He turned to Annie. "And what did you mean by 'training'?"

Robbie and Annie exchanged glances with an intimacy that Niall didn't like. Was there something between them? He felt a stab between the ribs that made him regret his precipitous decision to let go of the other man's throat.

Annie must have guessed some of Niall's thoughts because she stepped in front of Robbie, not realizing the additional damage she was doing to the young man's already-bruised pride.

"I'm not sure what concern it is of yours, but if you must know, Robbie is teaching me how to defend myself with a knife."

Niall had every intention of telling her what concern it was of his, but then he heard the word "knife." "He's doing *what*?"

He hadn't realized he'd shouted the last until

Annie's big green eyes flashed like a lightning storm, and she raised her own voice in reply. "You heard me—except apparently the part where it's none of your concern. Leave, Niall. You and your opinions are not welcome here."

She looked angry enough to mean it, and Niall realized his fear for her had gotten the better of him. He had to calm down. But anger and rage had ruled him for a long time. It had been a while since he'd behaved with any care for civility. Still, this wasn't how he intended this to go. He didn't want to fight with her. He wanted to apologize.

But damn it, she was a lass. Lasses didn't train with knives. Did she have any idea how many errant stabs and slices he'd suffered when Malcolm trained him?

Niall tried not to shudder and forced himself to take a different tack.

He addressed the red-faced lad-man behind her. "Would you give Annie and me a few minutes?" Considering the fact that he'd like nothing more than to rip the other man in two for putting her in such danger, Niall was rather proud of the semi-friendly tone he'd managed. Well, at least it wasn't outrightly hostile. "There is something I need to say to her in private."

"You and I have nothing to say to one another," Annie interjected with an impudent lift of her chin.

Her mouth was pursed so tightly Niall was tempted—far too tempted—to pull her into his arms and kiss the stubbornness from her face once and for all.

But he'd had years of experience in controlling

his attraction to her, which had been a hell of a lot harder when she'd looked at him as if he were a tasty treat that she couldn't wait to devour.

She wasn't looking at him at all like that now. The realization that she might not want him to kiss her hit him hard.

Robbie turned to her rather than respond directly to Niall. "I'll send him on his way if you want, but he's just going to keep coming around until you hear him out. If it's truly over, tell him. For all our sakes."

Their eyes held long enough for Niall to want to tear his gaze away. Finally, she nodded.

Robbie stepped away, but not before he got in the last word. He drew himself up to his full height—which might have been an inch or two taller than Niall's. As far as threatening and imposing went, it wasn't without effect. Which was surprising, given that Niall had him pressed up against a wall with one hand not five minutes before.

"Hurt her again, and I will hunt you down," Robbie said darkly. "And unlike the king's men, I will find you."

Niall quirked his brow, giving a slight challenge to the threat, but Robbie was already walking away.

Unfortunately, Niall wasn't the only one watching him. Annie's gaze was also on the other man. She was frowning in a perplexed way that made Niall uneasy. It was as if she were seeing Robbie in a way that she hadn't before and didn't know what to make of it.

Niall didn't want her to make anything of it. She loved *him*. Although it was hard to see that right now.

With the frown still on her face, she turned back to Niall and crossed her arms. He couldn't tell whether it was with boredom or disdain—neither of which was particularly welcome at the moment.

"Say what you have to say and then leave. For good this time."

How someone who was wearing clothes the scullery maid wouldn't be seen in and looked as if she'd been rolling in the dirt could look so bloody imperious, he didn't know. Neither did he understand how a mussed braid, a smudged nose, and flushed-with-work cheeks could be so stunningly beautiful.

But she took his breath away. Literally.

Niall had been waiting over a year for this moment, but it was as if someone had grabbed him by the throat. The emotion, the feelings, the despair, the horror… they all came back to him at once. He was overwhelmed by the force of it. By the import.

How could he explain how sorry he was? How much she meant to him? How much of a mistake he'd made? How he'd give anything in the world to take it all back? How he'd spent most of the past winter and spring doing everything he could to bring her justice?

He took in every inch of her face, gorging like a man who'd been starved of details and wanting to consign every one of them to memory forever. How could he have forgotten the precise arch of her brows? Or the way her dark, feathery lashes seemed to brush the corner of her eyes like the wing of a bird? Or the shimmery flecks of silver in her eyes, the smooth creaminess of her skin—even beneath the dirt—and the ripe red of a mouth that was far more sensual than he'd allowed himself to remember?

How many times had he dreamed of her, dreamed of this moment? And now that it was here, he didn't know what to do. What to say. How could he convey the sheer depth of his regret?

His words—like his thoughts—were out of order, and he started where he wanted to end. He took her by the arm and drew her closer. Not close enough for their bodies to touch, but close enough for her to know that he meant every word he was about to say.

"You don't need to learn how to defend yourself, Annie. Marry me, and I'll protect you for the rest of my life."

ANNIE STARED AT THE MAN WHO SEEMED A stranger to her. It wasn't just his looks that had changed. She used to think that no one knew her better than Niall Lamont. But this man didn't understand her at all. If he did, he would know exactly why this was so important to her.

She peered up at him, taking in the hard jaw that was dark with a week's worth of beard, the eyes that could rival any precious stones, the new lines etched around them, and the handful of nicks and small scars that marked his otherwise flawless face.

There wasn't anything she could find wrong with his features. His nose was perfectly proportioned and straight, his brow broad and high, his jaw fixed with just the right amount of masculine squareness, his mouth full and well curved, his eyes brilliant and tilted with an angle of hooded intensity. His dark, almost black hair was longer now and fell just past his jaw in silky waves.

The roguish grin and teasing lightness might have been replaced by a dark edginess and aura of danger, but Niall Lamont was still one of the most handsome men she'd ever beheld.

But if his looks used to make her breath catch, it was the way he'd seemed to be able to read her mind that had made her think they were destined for one another.

How could she have been so wrong?

Surprisingly, she hadn't flinched when he touched her, but the warm imprint of his fingers around her arm was not a welcome sensation, and she stared at his hand until he let it drop.

An uncomfortable silence fell between them for a few moments. Something that had never happened before Dunvegan. It seemed one more harsh reminder of how much everything had changed, and she didn't hesitate to refuse the awkward proposal that at one time she would have given her eyeteeth to hear.

"I do not want to marry you, Niall. Nor do I want or need your 'protection.' You seem to have taken it upon yourself to act as my executioner, but I want it to stop. You do not speak for me, nor do you have any right to seek justice for me. You had no right to kill Colin Campbell."

His face darkened with a malevolence that she would never have imagined him capable of. "I had every right. He hurt the woman I love. My only regret is that I could not prolong his agony before my sword took his foul life."

Annie ignored the tiny blip in the beating of her heart at the easy mention of the word "love." He was obviously confusing it with pity.

Still, she was curious about his choice of words. "Could not?"

His gaze bore into hers with a ferocity that almost made her gasp. "I gave my word to his brother that I would end it quickly."

Annie knew that Niall's sister had married Colin's younger brother. "The Enforcer?" she asked, referring to Jamie Campbell.

Niall shook his head. "Duncan Campbell. The older brother that Colin had attempted to kill to prevent Duncan inheriting the lordship that Colin had wrongfully claimed."

Annie nodded. Patrick had mentioned something about it, but she hadn't been listening very closely. She'd been too angry at Niall for claiming the justice that should have belonged to her.

"You overstepped your bounds, Niall. You and I are nothing to one another. We haven't been for over two years."

"God, I'm sorry, Annie. You have no idea how much I regret what I said at Dunvegan. If I could take it all back, I would. It didn't take me long to realize I'd made a mistake. I was going to find you and apologize, but then war broke out. Ascog was attacked, my father and brother killed, your kinsmen betrayed by Argyll, and you were—"

She held up her hand and cut him off. She knew; she didn't need to hear it from him. "It doesn't matter. An apology wouldn't have made a difference."

"Of course it would have. How can you say that? You loved me."

She looked him straight in the eye. "I did. With all my heart. But after what happened, I realized I had given my heart away too easily to someone who didn't deserve it."

He looked as if she'd shot him with a hagbut in the gut. His face drained of most of its color. "I was one and twenty, Annie. I was inexperienced and didn't know what I wanted. I didn't know that what I felt for you was special."

She couldn't quite bite back all the sarcasm when she said, "You weren't that inexperienced from what I heard."

He actually flushed. If Annie didn't know better, she'd think he was ashamed. "I was a fool. I didn't realize how lucky I was to have found the woman I loved when I was fourteen. I convinced myself that what I felt for you didn't matter. I thought I was doing my duty. I thought I was being a man."

He sounded sincere, but Annie didn't want to hear any of this. It was too late. Too many things had changed. Including her. *Especially* her.

She hadn't realized how much until that moment. Standing this close to Niall two years ago, she would have been buzzing all over. She would have been flush with anticipation, the hairs on her arms would have been standing on edge, and she would have been warm and achy. She would have been planning ways to get him to kiss her.

She would have felt desire.

But now she felt... nothing. Not one little stirring of anything. Not even Niall—the man she'd practically thrown herself at for two years—could make her feel again. The passion of the one kiss they'd shared had haunted her. She'd hoped at some point that that part of her would return.

The realization of all that she'd lost—of all that had been taken from her—made her want to cry. For the first time since those awful initial weeks, tears sprang to her eyes.

He obviously misunderstood. "Jesus, Annie, I didn't mean to make you upset. I just wanted to tell you how sorry I was and how much I love you and want to make it up to you."

It was the wrong thing to say. "Make it up to me? God, do you have any idea how ridiculous that sounds? Not everything can be 'made up,' Niall. Not everything can be fixed. When some things are broken, they stay that way forever."

He was clearly taken aback by her vehemence. "I'm sorry. I didn't mean to speak lightly—"

"No. You just think you can stride in here, tell me you love me, and magically make it all be better. Well, it's *never* going to be better, Niall. It's too late. And the best thing you can do for me—the *only* thing you can do—is leave me be."

She turned and fled before he could see the tears that were now streaming down her cheeks.

CHAPTER THREE

NIALL MUTTERED A HARSH CURSE as Annie fled across the *barmkin*. How the hell had that gone so wrong?

He debated for a moment whether to go after her but didn't want to make things worse. And until he figured out where he'd gone wrong, there was every likelihood of that happening.

He was about to sit down on a stack of hay to try to gather his thoughts when he saw a man stalking toward him.

He cursed again. Great, just what he needed: an angry—make that irate—brother who looked as if he wanted to take Niall's head off.

The fact that Patrick MacGregor, Chief of Mac-Gregor, was one of the few men who could actually do that made it even worse.

"I thought I told you to stay away from her," Patrick bit out as his fist connected with Niall's jaw.

Niall didn't attempt to block the blow and groaned as something akin to the force of a sledge-hammer snapped his head back. He blinked stars as he tried to lunge out of the way to evade the next blow.

He didn't quite make it, and an equally powerful left fist connected with his stomach—and a few ribs. Niall's thick leather jack probably prevented bones from breaking, but it didn't stop the air from being expelled from his lungs in an "oof" or the grunt of pain that followed.

Christ, Annie's brother's reputation for nearly inhuman strength was well earned.

Niall was bent over from the second blow when Patrick paused before him. Only the fact that Niall wasn't fighting back probably stopped a third blow from knocking him out cold. Instead, Patrick lifted Niall up by the scruff and held him a good foot off the ground. The irony of Niall being in the opposite position with Robbie a short while before didn't escape him.

"Give me one good reason why I shouldn't thrash you within an inch of your life. I told you to stay the hell away from her!"

"I did—or I meant to," Niall explained. "But as I was leaving, I saw her on the ground with someone on top of her. She was thrashing around and trying to get him off."

Patrick let him go. "Someone attacked her in the castle?"

Niall shook his head. "I assumed the man was hurting her and almost killed him before I learned they were training." It was his turn to be furious. "What in Hades were you thinking, allowing a lass to train with a knife? She could be hurt—or killed!"

Patrick's expression lost some of its fierceness. "The man on top of her was Robbie." It was a realization not a question. He muttered a coarse curse.

Niall agreed. "Apparently Annie forgot where she was for a moment and didn't realize it was Robbie."

Patrick swore again. "Is that why she was so upset?"

Niall grimaced and wisely took a step back—out of range of Patrick's fist. "Not exactly. I took the opportunity to apologize and ask her to marry me, but it didn't go as I planned."

Patrick's expression darkened again. "Meaning she refused you. Damn it, I told you she wasn't ready."

"I guess you were right. I just thought if I explained…" Niall's voice dropped off, and he finished with a repentant shrug.

"What? That she'd forgive and forget and jump back into your arms? You're either an idiot or an arrogant arse."

Niall wanted to argue, but he feared the other man might be right on both counts. His shoulders slumped, all the fight going out of him. "I don't know what I thought, but you were right: Annie has changed."

She was harder and far more serious—almost solemn. The spirited, slightly mischievous girl whose smile had filled him with instant joy was gone. He probably should have expected it after all that had happened, but he could never have anticipated the cold indifference in the way she'd looked at him. He was so used to seeing her heart in her eyes he'd taken it for granted that it would always be there.

It *was* still there. It had to be. He just had to find a way to convince her to give him another chance and forgive him for failing her so miserably.

Patrick's anger was directed at him again. He took a step toward him, fists clenching at his side. "There is nothing wrong with her."

Niall stood his ground. Patrick had obviously misunderstood his words and taken them as a criticism. It made him wonder whether her brother had heard something like that before. The idea that Annie might have been the subject of comment and gossip infuriated him as much as it did Patrick.

"Of course there isn't. My estimation for her has only increased. I always knew she was as strong and tough as she was beautiful, but I didn't realize the depth. I was just taken aback by the change in her temperament. She used to be so…"

He didn't need to finish. Patrick understood. He appeared just as saddened by the change as Niall. "Given what she's been through, can you blame her? All things considered, I think she's doing remarkably well. You just have to be patient."

Why did Niall suspect that Patrick had said the same thing to himself many times?

"I'm trying but…" He stopped.

"But what?"

Niall debated how to respond. He didn't want to put Patrick in a bad position with his Campbell brothers-in-law. "I might not have much time. My circumstances are a little… uncertain."

The other man's eyes narrowed. "I thought Argyll intended to look the other way about your killing Colin Campbell."

"He has."

Patrick knew he was hedging. "But?"

"Before he died, I persuaded Colin Campbell to

tell me the three names."

Patrick swore with comprehension. "So that's what you've been doing, tracking down the men who raped her? My brothers-in-law and their cousin Argyll are going to be furious. They took a big risk for you with the king. Jamie Campbell took surety for you, as I recall."

Niall's jaw hardened. He knew what Jamie had done in taking personal responsibility for him—and he felt badly about it—but it wasn't as if Niall had a choice. "Would you be doing any differently?"

Patrick gave him a look of disgust but didn't bother to answer. They both knew he would be first in line behind him.

"Annie is going to be furious when she finds out. She was mad enough about your killing Colin Campbell."

Niall frowned. "I would think she would want justice."

"She does," Patrick said dryly. "She just wants it to come from her hand. My sister has more Mac-Gregor in her than I realized."

Niall suddenly understood and gaped at him in horror. "Good God! You aren't actually supporting this madness? You can't mean to train her with a knife to allow her to go after the men who raped her?"

The two who were left, that is.

"Of course not," Patrick said with disgust. "But unlike you, I know when not to get in her way. She was going to learn to use a knife whether I authorized it or not. This way at least I could make sure she did so safely with someone who would die rather than see her hurt."

Niall didn't like hearing *that* at all. "After what I saw today, I'd be surprised if those lessons continue. They both looked horrified by what happened."

Patrick shook his head. "I warned her that it wasn't a good idea—for either of them. But I have to admit she surprised me. From what I saw, she wasn't bad."

Niall figured that was a bit of brotherly exaggeration.

Patrick shrugged and continued. "When I thought about it, I realized learning to defend herself wasn't a completely irrational idea under the circumstances. No matter how much I wish it, I can't always be there to protect her. Besides, I think she needs to do this—for herself."

Niall was afraid he understood exactly what Patrick meant because he knew Annie. Which didn't make him happy right now. She didn't trust anyone to protect her. She didn't trust him or Patrick or any other man whom she should have been able to count on. And why should she? They'd let her down.

Guilt squeezed his chest so intensely it was hard to breathe.

But even understanding where the need came from, it chilled him to think of the trouble she could get in if she pulled a blade on the wrong person or, worse, actually did try to go after the Campbell soldiers who'd raped her.

"If anyone should be training her, it should be me," Niall said grimly.

Patrick laughed but didn't disagree. "Good luck convincing her of that. And even if you could, given what you just told me, why should I allow it? Your situation on the wrong side of the law hasn't exactly improved. Do you think I want my sister being hunted by the king's men?"

"It won't come to that."

"If you are counting on Jamie Campbell to intercede on your behalf with Argyll again, I think you are overestimating your sister's influence."

"You obviously don't know my sister very well." It wasn't Caitrina's influence with her husband that he worried about; it was her annoyance with Niall for putting her husband in a bad position. But he wasn't going to tell Patrick MacGregor that. "If all else fails, I have a plan. Annie will not be in harm's way. Do you think I'd be here if it were any other way?"

"That still doesn't explain how you are going to convince her to agree to let you train her. She doesn't want to see you."

"Let me worry about that."

If Niall sounded more confident than he felt, he hid it well. He just hoped he knew Annie as well as he thought he did.

WANTING TO AVOID PRYING EYES AND QUEST-ions, Annie didn't return to the castle right away. Instead she hid out in a secluded corner of the garden until she could collect herself and dry her tears before returning to her chamber.

"Black" Duncan Campbell might be a murdering despot, but Annie had to admit that he did know how to build a modern castle. She had been too young to remember the old MacGregor keep as it had been when her parents were alive, but she knew it was nothing like the massive, modern Z-plan tower house that Black Duncan had built on its ruins. The center of the *z* was a three-story rectangular-shaped tower that housed the great hall, kitchens, and other private solars. On opposite corners of the central tower were two four-story round tower houses that added a dozen rooms for family, household servants, and guards.

Annie had never had her own chamber before and was surprised at how quickly she'd grown to enjoy the solitude that was otherwise difficult to find in a busy and crowded castle. With the servants, attendants, retainers, skilled laborers, and her brother's garrison of soldiers—both Campbell and MacGregor—there were over fifty people living at Edinample Castle, and many more workers, merchants, and villagers coming in and out throughout the day.

It didn't take long for her secluded corner in the garden to be invaded by two young serving girls gathering vegetables and herbs for the midday meal, forcing Annie from her hiding place.

She wiped her eyes, angry at herself for the loss of composure—both with Robbie and with Niall. She would be better prepared next time. If there was a next time. With any luck, Niall would disappear back into that dark mist that he'd emerged from, and Robbie...

Her heart squeezed. What was she going to do about Robbie?

She would have to talk to him tomorrow. Right now all she wanted to do was call for a tub of hot water, soak in it until the water turned cold, and then curl up in her bed for a nap that with any luck would last the rest of the day.

Unfortunately, the only entrance to the castle was through a small door tucked into the corner where the southeast circular tower and main tower house met. It was good for defense, but not, as it turned out, good for evading well-meaning relatives.

"There you are," Elizabeth said, looking up from where she was seated with the baby and her maid-servant in the great hall as Annie attempted to dart to the opposite tower where her third-story chamber was housed. "Alys and I were going to walk into the village later, and I wondered if you would watch…" Her voice dropped off as she scanned Annie's face. "Oh my goodness, what happened? Are you hurt?"

"I'm fine," Annie said automatically, forgetting how perceptive her sister by marriage could be.

Elizabeth Campbell might be quiet and reserved most of the time, but she watched and listened to people closely. Annie knew she had a stammer, and she suspected that was part of the reason.

As a result, all that Annie's quick denial succeeded in doing was increase her scrutiny. Elizabeth—Lizzie, as she insisted Annie call her—took in the vestiges of puffy, red-rimmed eyes, mottled cheeks, and a nose that was raw from wiping. "You are not fine," Lizzie said, standing up and handing the baby she'd been holding to the older woman seated beside her. "What can I do?"

"Nothing," Annie insisted, wanting to crawl under a rock with embarrassment. "Really. I just…" Her voice dropped off, trying to think of an explanation. "I was training, and I fell."

It was sort of the truth.

And Lizzie sort of believed her. Or at least she chose to accept the explanation and not press.

Anticipating what Lizzie had been about to ask, Annie tried to change the subject. "I'd be happy to watch Iain later when you and Alys go into town."

Annie smiled at the pretty older woman who, if anything, seemed even more perceptive than her former charge. Not for the first time, Annie caught Alys watching her with compassion in Alys's gaze. But it wasn't just compassion, it was…

Annie couldn't quite put her finger on it.

Elizabeth shook her head. "That's all right. I can ask one of the serving girls—"

"Nonsense," Annie insisted, meaning it. "I'd love to spend the time with my nephew." It was just what she needed. Her nap could wait. Her bath could not. "Just let me get cleaned up, and I'll take him."

"If you are sure," Lizzie said skeptically. "Iain does seem to cry less when he is with you. We won't be long. Alys found some linens for the baby's cradle in the village but couldn't decide which color."

Annie suspected the fabrics were an excuse to force Lizzie outside the castle where she'd been "cooped up," as Alys told her, after the baby.

Annie hurried up to her room to call for the bath.

Not long after she emerged from the soothing waters—feeling much better—there was a knock on the door. Assuming it was one of the girls to take the tub away, she bid them enter.

She was surprised instead to see Alys.

Lizzie's former nursemaid and now loyal attendant had come to Edinample with her husband, a captain in the Campbell guard. The former MacGregor castle had been part of Lizzie's tocher, and Patrick had taken command on their marriage, but Jamie Campbell insisted that some of his guardsmen form the garrison.

Alys must be in her late thirties, but her light hair was still free of gray, and her classical features had a timeless beauty.

"Did I take too long?" Annie asked her. "I was just coming down to find you and Lizzie."

Alys shook her head. "Nay, I wanted to talk to you for a few minutes. Do you mind?"

"Of course not." Annie motioned for the older woman to sit on the chair before the brazier.

Annie sat opposite her on the edge of the bed while she finished dragging a comb through her still-damp hair. "What can I do for you?"

The other woman seemed uncomfortable, as if she didn't know what to say or was actually reconsidering her presence there at all.

Finally she spoke. "It's none of my business, and I hope you will forgive an old woman for her interference, but am I right to think that the handsome warrior who met with the laird earlier and bears an uncanny resemblance to Lizzie's new sister-in-law was the cause of your distress?"

Other than Patrick, Annie had never talked to anyone about Niall, and she wasn't inclined to start with a stranger. But she didn't want to be rude to the person who was like a mother to Lizzie, and Alys was looking at her so kindly that she found herself nodding. "He is Caitrina's brother."

"The outlawed brother, Niall, I'm guessing," Alys surmised. She nodded to herself. "I thought so."

Annie wondered where she was heading with this but was more eager to put an end to the subject. "If you are worried about having an outlaw around, you needn't worry. I've sent him away, and I will tell my brother to ensure—"

"No, no. That isn't it." Alys's clenched hands that were in her lap started to twist anxiously. "I'm sorry. I'm doing a horrible job of this. But I've heard something of Niall and also of what happened to you."

Annie stiffened reflexively. "I'm sure you have."

There was nothing that some people liked to do more than gossip, and the new laird's sister being raped on the orders of his new wife's now-dead brother would be too sensational to ignore.

Annie just wasn't used to having to address the gossip directly. It was usually done in whispers and exchanged knowing looks behind her back.

Realizing that she'd upset her, Alys reached out to take her hand and looked at her imploringly. "I just wanted to tell you that I understand."

Annie didn't know what she was trying to say, but the last thing she wanted or needed was someone else feeling sorry for her. She had enough of that with her immediate family.

"Thank you. I appreciate that."

She started to stand up, but Alys used her hand to hold her down. "No, I mean that I *understand*. I know what you are going through right now because I've been in the same place."

Taken aback, Annie didn't respond right away. But then she said, "You were…?"

Raped. She'd come to hate the word. Its harshness. Its finality. The way it branded and defined her. As if it had come to summarize everything that was now important about her.

Alys nodded. "Years ago. When I was about your age. I was newly married to Donnan who was a guardsman to the old Laird of Auchinbreck at the time. My father was the Chief of Buchanan, and to marry my Donnan, I refused a powerful chieftain whom my father had hoped I would wed."

Annie stared at her wordlessly. Lizzie's nursemaid was the daughter of a Highland chief? She'd married well below her station to accept the hand of a mere guardsman.

"The chieftain didn't take my refusal well," Alys continued. "He hoped to get his revenge by humiliating my father and husband and forcing them into a war that they would have lost. I was his means of revenge."

Annie knew exactly what she meant and didn't know what to say. *Crossfire.* "I'm sorry."

Alys waved her off. "It was a long time ago. The years of happiness I have had since then far outweigh the horror of what that man did to me. That is why I am here."

Annie frowned. "I don't understand."

Alys seemed to put aside her reticence once and for all and looked her straight in the eye. "If that man loves you as much as I think he does and you still love him, you need to try to work through this. Do not sacrifice your future happiness for today's pain. Do not let those men take away the happiness you deserve."

Annie tried not to bristle. "You don't understand.

It's not that simple."

"You are right. I don't know all the facts, but I do know how you are feeling right now, and I can tell you it won't always be that way. It gets better—especially if you have a man whom you love to help you."

But hadn't she just had proved that things would never be the same? "I don't love him—not anymore at least."

"Are you sure about that?"

Alys let the question sit there for a moment before getting to her feet. "I've interfered enough. But I would never have forgiven myself if I'd stayed silent when I might have been able to prevent a second tragedy." She paused, looking embarrassed. "I would appreciate it if you wouldn't say anything about what I've told you. No one knows."

"Of course," Annie said. "You were fortunate to avoid gossip and not have the cause for the war leak out."

"There was no war," Alys said quietly. "I never told anyone."

Annie's eyes widened. "Not even your husband?"

Alys shook her head. "That was what the chieftain wanted. He wanted Donnan to challenge him so he could kill him."

"And Donnan never found out?"

"No. Even after the chieftain died a few months later—he ate something that didn't agree with him, I believe—I was afraid to tell him."

"Why? The threat was gone."

"I wasn't sure…" Her voice dropped off, and she seemed to be very far away. After a few moments, the older woman smiled wistfully. "I wasn't as fortunate as you."

Me, fortunate? "What do you mean?"

"Highland warriors are a proud lot. Your Niall knows what those men did to you and doesn't care. He still loves you and wants you. I wasn't sure if my Donnan found out that he would ever be able to look at me the same."

CHAPTER FOUR

A LYS HAD GIVEN ANNIE A lot to think about. More than she wanted to, actually. She was stunned that the older woman had kept something like that to herself for all these years.

For the first time, Annie realized how fortunate she was to have a family and friends who loved her, supported her, and worried about her—even if their "cosseting" could sometimes drive her half-crazed.

She could be as alone as Alys had been.

Last night at the evening meal, Annie couldn't help watching Lizzie's maidservant with her husband. She suspected Alys was wrong about one thing: her husband wouldn't have stopped loving her if he'd known. Donnan Campbell very clearly adored his wife. Annie could see the love in his eyes as he looked at Alys even from halfway across the room.

Annie could only hope that one day someone would look at her like that.

Someone already did.

She pushed the unwelcome thought away, but it wasn't the first time that she'd thought of the way

Niall had been looking at her yesterday.

She didn't know what she expected. Pity maybe? Guilt? At the very least, she'd thought he'd look at her differently.

But Niall looked at her the same way he always did, except that it was perhaps more intense. She wanted to ascribe it to the change in Niall himself—he was certainly much more intense—but she knew there was more to it. His eyes had fixed on her as if he'd been starving for the sight of her. As if she meant something—everything—to him. As if her forgiveness was the most important thing in the world to him.

As if the past two years had never happened.

He still wanted her. And maybe that had surprised her a little. Most men wouldn't after what had been done to her. Even if they realized it wasn't her fault, she was somehow tainted. Impure. Sullied. The unfairness of that was one more injustice forced on her.

But he didn't get to look at her like that. Not after humiliating her and breaking her heart.

"I can't marry you."

The memory was forever burned into her consciousness in the way that only a skin-crawling humiliation could be. No matter what Niall claimed now, Annie didn't believe him. Actions were what mattered to her, and if Niall had truly loved her, he never would have been able to hurt her like that.

Guilt was obviously a powerful motivator.

Besides, she was over him. Yesterday had proved that. He might still want her, but she no longer wanted him.

It was only natural that her thoughts kept drifting back to yesterday and that she kept picturing all the changes in him. It certainly didn't matter— nor was it any of her business—how he'd gotten all those new scars. So what if his dark hair was longer and he didn't seem to shave very often anymore? And what could it possibly matter if his arms were a good three inches thicker in muscle?

Those kinds of details no longer concerned her.

She had to remind herself of that quite a few times after breaking her fast while she waited for Robbie in their makeshift practice yard near the stables. She passed the time tossing her wooden knife at a coiled straw mat in the shape of a targe that had been tied to a post for the squires to practice their archery. Her practice blade didn't stick like a real knife would, but it was fun to see how close she could get to the middle of the hastily painted concentric circles.

Really close. In fact, twice she sent the point of the blade very near the center.

She was about to go for number three when she started at a sharp whizzing sound going past her head on the left. It was followed by a hard thud as a blade stuck in the precise center of the targe.

She spun around, intending to scold Robbie for startling her—and for being late—but stopped (or perhaps froze was the better word) when she saw the man standing about twenty feet behind her. The man who wasn't Robbie.

"You throw well," he said, closing the distance between them in a few long strides.

Her mouth pursed in a thin line. Not at his tone, which was matter-of-fact rather than surprised, but at his presence.

"I thought I told you to go away."

He ignored her decidedly *un*pleasantry. "Your aim would be more consistent if you started your hand more up by your ear with the blade pointed behind you. But your follow-through is good. And you put your weight into it. Young MacGregor taught you well."

"Robbie didn't teach me. I just started doing it on my own to pass the time. Like the squires," she added.

He nodded as if that made sense. But before he could respond and attempt to distract her again, which had no doubt been what he was doing by intriguing her with almost praise and instruction, she slid the practice knife back into the scabbard that Robbie had fashioned for her at her thigh. If she noticed the way his gaze dipped to her leg and lingered, she didn't show it. The warmth in her cheeks was clearly from the sun.

She crossed her arms in front of her chest impatiently. "Why are you here, Niall?"

He looked into her eyes, penetrating into places where he didn't belong. Deep places. Buried places. "You know why."

Had his voice always been that rich and husky? That warm and seductive? As if it could wrap around her like a soft plaid?

Yes.

It used to make her skin prickle and send shivers racing up and down her spine. Even now she felt a tickle at the back of her neck and the hairs on her arms seemed to be standing on end.

She frowned—scowled—though whether at

him or herself, she didn't know. "And as I told you yesterday, it's impossible."

It was too late.

"Prove it."

She blinked her widened eyes more than once. "What?"

"I said prove it. Give me a month. If you still feel the same, I will do as you ask and leave you alone."

She stared at him, hearing what he hadn't said. "For good?"

He hesitated. "For good," he repeated with a nod.

NIALL HOPED HE KNEW WHAT HE WAS DOING. He'd never been much of a gambler, but he was risking everything on this. He better know her as well as he thought he did. Annie was stubborn, but she could also never resist a challenge—especially when her pride was at stake.

He felt her eyes scanning his face and tried not to react or show how anxious he was. But he wondered if she saw it anyway. She seemed to guess what he was about.

She shook her head. "No." And then another repeated more forcefully, "No. I won't change my mind whether it is a month or a year."

"Then you have nothing to lose," he persisted. "Besides, you need someone to train you if you want to learn to defend yourself with a knife. Throwing at targets is fun for practice, but it isn't anything you would want to do in a real attack."

"Why?"

"It would be a rare occurrence that you would

want to throw away your only weapon."

She pursed her pretty lips together, clearly angry with herself for letting him distract her with talk of training. "I don't need your help. I have an instructor."

He might have smiled. "You mean you *had* an instructor."

Vestiges of the old Annie returned when her eyes flashed with fury. It shouldn't make him so happy, but he felt the first flickers of hope stirring inside his chest. "What did you do to him, Niall? I swear if you hurt him, I will see that you—"

"I didn't do anything to him," he assured her before she could start issuing her threats.

Clearly, she didn't believe him. "Tell me Robbie isn't lying somewhere tied up or locked in some cellar nursing his wounds."

His mouth curved very slowly. "I wouldn't do something like that."

She pressed one finger to his chest and tapped without realizing what she was doing. "You would do a lot worse. I know exactly what kind of foul tricks you are capable of. You and my brother were always making trouble."

She stopped suddenly, pulling back her hand and letting it drop. Horror filled her gaze and made his chest squeeze.

"I miss him, too, Annie." Her stare was stark and empty, but he could feel her pain. "I'm sorry," he added.

She nodded and averted her face as if she didn't want him to see her hurt when all he wanted to do was take it away. He had to resist the urge to reach for her, something that he never would have thought of before. She'd always welcomed his touch. More than welcomed. She'd basked in it like a kitten stretching in the sun.

But he sensed that it was too soon for that kind of intimacy, and worse, that she might not welcome it.

He had to be patient. But that wasn't a virtue that came naturally to him, especially when it was warring with his desperation to reforge the connection between them as soon as possible. Like in the next minute.

"Robbie is fine," he assured her. She gave him a very suspicious sidelong glance. "At least I assume he is, as I haven't seen him since he left this morning."

Her eyes narrowed. "Where did he go so suddenly, and why am I only hearing about this now?"

Niall shrugged. "I don't know. You'll have to ask your brother. But I think he volunteered to take some silver to your clansmen on Molach." He paused. "I suspect he was eager to be away for a few days."

She couldn't hide her disappointment. "I don't understand. Why would he be eager to leave?"

Niall arched his brow. "Can you not think of a reason?"

The hot pink flush that rose to her cheeks suggested she could. "It was a misunderstanding. Robbie knows that."

"I'm sure he does. Just like you know what the real problem is." She looked down, hiding her discomfort by brushing nonexistent dirt from her *leine*. He hesitated but took the chance and reached down to lift her chin with the back of his finger.

She didn't flinch, which felt like a major victory. "You know that you can't continue practicing with the lad. It isn't fair to him."

She wrenched away. Perhaps realizing that he was touching her or perhaps because she didn't like what he said.

But he proved that he did know her well when instead of objecting, she just clamped her mouth down with the mulish expression that he remembered. After a moment of stewing, she glared at him. "He isn't a lad. And it's no business of yours."

It sure as hell was. The only man she was going to roll around in the dirt with was him—even if he had to temporarily disable every guardsman in the castle. But instead of pointing that out, he smiled. "I thought you were interested in learning how to defend yourself?"

She lifted her chin defiantly. "I am."

"You have another instructor in mind?"

"I'm sure I can find someone."

"Even if you can, they won't be as good as me."

"Still arrogant, I see."

He shrugged. "It's not arrogance when it's the truth. Ask anyone."

"I don't need to."

He grinned. "Been listening to stories about me, have you?"

She snorted. "I meant that your skill doesn't matter, as you won't be instructing me in anything."

He shrugged as if it didn't matter either way. "It's up to you. But I'll have to find some other way to pass the boredom for the next month."

"I didn't agree to that."

"I thought you said it wouldn't matter 'whether

it was a month or a year.'"

"It wouldn't."

"Then what's the problem?"

Her frustration was obviously getting to her, as he thought she might have stomped her foot. "You are an outlaw, for one. What if someone discovers you are here?"

His mouth curved in a half smile. "The custom of Highland hospitality goes both ways. And the Campbell guardsmen think I'm a Murray."

"So you manipulated my brother into letting you stay here with guilt for what happened with your father?"

He would have if he'd had to. "I merely asked for temporary refuge, and he granted it."

"Because you knew he could not refuse!"

He shrugged as if the distinction made no difference to him—it didn't. "If your only problem is concern for me, then why not agree? You can prove to me that it's over and have one of the best instructors in the Highlands at your disposal for the next four weeks."

He thought he detected the tiniest glimmer of possibility in her eye. But his Annie was a stubborn lass.

Her eyes were blazing hot enough to start a fire. "I'm not concerned for you, and I don't need to prove anything."

"Maybe not, but do you have so many men lining up to teach you skill with a blade that you can afford to refuse one who is right here and willing to help?"

He could see from the wavering in her eyes that he'd struck gold on that one. But he didn't press his advantage. He didn't need to. She would come around on her own.

Patience.

ANNIE HELD OUT FOR THREE DAYS. SHE DIDN'T realize how much she'd come to look forward to the training sessions with Robbie, but now that they were gone, she felt restless. The mornings of outdoor activity and exercise made the days without that which followed in the castle seem stifling and restricting. She felt as if she'd been locked in a closet.

Of course, she could have gone outside the castle, but *he* was there. Taunting her, the wretch. She knew it wasn't a mistake that Niall happened to train with her brother and his guardsmen in perfect view of wherever she happened to be. She could no longer knit or embroider anywhere near a window without hearing the ruckus of steel on steel as the men sparred in various areas of the *barmkin*. The boom of his laugh or the deep resonance of his voice followed her everywhere.

Even her nephew conspired against her. Iain had been crying a lot of late, and Lizzie discovered that he quieted when she brought him by the door or window of the great hall to watch his father practice. She thought it was the noise or the flash of swords and men that distracted him.

It was distracting all right. And infuriating. Annie knew Niall was manipulating her by offering her something that would prove too tempting to refuse. She tried to go around him by finding someone else, but she might as well have been asking for help cleaning a cesspit. That was the reaction she got from her brother's men who were all "too busy." Her brother just told her to stop being so stubborn and take Niall up on his offer—didn't she realize what an honor it was?—or just wait for Robbie to return.

But Niall had been right about that as well—blast him again. She'd known even before he made his Trojan gift offer that she couldn't keep training with Robbie. It wasn't fair to use him like that when she knew his feelings for her hadn't changed.

Niall, however, she had no qualms about using. She'd meant it when she'd told him a month wouldn't make a difference. If he was hurt in the end, it would be his own fault.

She was angry enough at his manipulation to admit that she might even be looking forward to that moment.

On Wednesday morning, she stomped across the courtyard to where her tormentor was lazily tossing knives into the target from an obscene distance with an appalling degree of accuracy. It was almost as if he knew she was coming and was waiting for her. One knowing look or "I got you" smile and she would have spun on her heel and stomped away. But perhaps he had matured in the past few years. Even if she *knew* he was feeling that way inside, his expression was blank.

She stopped when she was within a few feet of him. Something slammed against her ribs, and she had the horrible suspicion that it was her heart. It wasn't slamming in the way it used to, with excitement and anticipation, but with something more troubling. It was a depth of awareness falling into place that she didn't like.

It must be because he was so changed, she told herself. It wasn't just the muscles or his size—he was nearly as big as Patrick now—or the scars and lines on his face. It was the aura that surrounded him. He'd become formidable.

The roguish boy had become an imposing man. She wasn't sure she liked it, but there was nothing that she could do about it. What was done was done. She, better than anyone, knew that.

"One week," she said. "I will give you one week, and if I want you to leave, you will promise me that you will go."

"Two," he said stonily.

"This isn't a negotiation, Niall. You and I both know that if I go to my brother, you will be escorted out of here by the tip of his sword, Highland hospitality or not." He didn't argue with her. "One week," she repeated.

He considered her for a moment, taking special care to let her know that he'd noticed her attire. "Very well, but I'm confident enough in my abilities to know that at the end of the week you will want more." She didn't miss the suggestiveness of his words, and he smiled. "Want more of my *training* abilities. Unless, of course, you ask me to leave for another reason."

"What other reason?"

He shrugged, but she knew exactly what he meant. He thought she would run scared because she wasn't as over him as she wanted to be. Well, he was completely wrong about that.

"I'm agreeing to let you train me for one week,

Niall, nothing else. You understand that, don't you?"

"Perfectly."

She didn't believe him.

"Good." She sniffed in the air. What was that blasted smell? It seemed to be wafting all around her like a warm, drugging bath.

"Did you roll around in pine needles or something?"

He arched one eyebrow. There was nothing wicked about it, but somehow it was exactly that. "It's my soap. You used to love the smell of the forests."

She didn't need to say anything about the wintry birch twigs on his breath that she smelled, too. He knew exactly how much she used to like that, too.

"It won't work, Niall. I've changed."

"We've all changed, Annie. You aren't the only one who has suffered the past two years."

Annie felt a sharp stab of conscience. Some of her anger and annoyance with him dissipated. He was right. She should have said something before. "I'm sorry about your father and brother. I liked Malcolm. He was always kind to me."

Niall looked away, silent for a moment, as if the memories were too much for him. Finally, he turned to her with a sharp nod. "He knew how I felt about you. Maybe better than I did myself. I miss them both."

Suddenly something occurred to her. Something she'd not wanted to think about, but now that she was here standing before him, she couldn't escape. "I would understand if you blame my clan for their deaths. I know they died protecting my kinsmen who'd taken refuge on your land."

His mouth fell in a hard line until tiny lines of white appeared around his lips. "There was only one person to blame for what happened to my family, and that was Colin Campbell." He practically spat the name. "I had more reason than one to see him dead."

Their eyes held, and for the first time in a long time, Annie felt as if someone understood her hatred and she didn't need to shy from it.

She was not ready to forgive him completely for taking her vengeance from her, but maybe she could understand why he'd done it. His need was as powerful as her own. But something needed to be clear.

"I want you to promise me that your days as my personal avenger are over. Any justice meted out in my name is mine to decide." He looked ready to argue, but she stopped him. "I mean it, Niall. You have done enough. Do you promise?"

His mouth pressed in a tight, grim line, and his eyes darkened. She could see that he did not want to agree, but he obviously read her determination and finally nodded.

Annie smiled. "Should we begin then?"

"If you are ready?"

She was. She couldn't wait to get started again.

CHAPTER FIVE

STARTING AGAIN IS EXACTLY WHAT happened. They went back to the beginning. And if Annie thought Robbie was methodical and slow to get to the good stuff, Niall was even more so.

For the next few days, they repeated the same basic lessons she'd had from Robbie in even more excruciating detail. Where Robbie made her do something a dozen times, Niall made her do it *two* dozen times before she could move on to the next step.

Five days later, she was still using the blasted wooden knife, and now she didn't just know how to remove it with her right hand—and hold the grip a variety of ways—she could do it with her left as well.

Initially suspicious of Niall's motives in agreeing to train her, Annie's wariness gradually relaxed after the first few days of instruction. He obviously took training—even training a woman—very seriously.

He wasn't cruel or unduly harsh, but neither was he particularly forgiving or understanding of her mistakes. Where Robbie had been tentative and patient to a painful fault, Niall was serious—even stern at times—and demanding. He suffered no excuses and gave no quarter. At times she wondered if he forgot she was a woman.

Annie loved every moment of it. It was exactly what she needed. She didn't want to be coddled or treated like a delicate flower. Niall's attitude was refreshing. And the challenge of the training invigorated her. It didn't just give her something to do—something that felt important—it also made her feel strong.

She'd been so powerless when those men attacked her. Learning to use a knife made it seem as if she was taking some of it back.

Although she couldn't be sure—Niall's expression was so frustratingly unreadable—she thought that her hard work and improving skills had impressed him. In the beginning, he hadn't seemed to be humoring her *exactly*, but with each day that passed, he seemed to be not just more comfortable with the idea but to have actually embraced it.

Maybe a little too much.

On the morning of their sixth day of practice, he gave her a new instruction.

She looked at him blankly and blinked a few times. "You want me to do what?"

"Run around the *barmkin* for a quarter of an hour or so to get warmed up."

Annie had run around the moors and braes of Glenlyon as a child, but that was some time ago. A quarter of an hour sounded like a long time. "I'm already warmed up," she said. "It's going to be another beautiful day, and I got out here early to practice that technique you showed me yesterday to throw the knife at the target with spin. It's better for warfare, right?"

She purposefully got it wrong, but he wasn't easily distracted. "Without spin. Now get running, Annie."

She made a face. "What does running have to do with knowing how to use a knife?"

He frowned as if he wasn't used to explaining himself and wasn't particularly enjoying the experience. "It will improve your endurance and make you stronger."

"I'm already strong."

"For a lass, maybe." He knew perfectly well how much she would hate that. "But even my weakest squire can run for an hour without trouble." He shrugged. "If you can't handle it…"

She muttered something foul under her breath and cut him off. "I didn't say I couldn't handle it."

"Good. Then get going. I'll tell you when to stop."

The first time around the yard wasn't too bad. The second time she was breathing hard. By the third, fourth, and fifth, she was really struggling, and by the sixth, she thought she was going to die. Fortunately, she was saved the humiliation of crawling for the seventh when Niall—from his lie-back-with-nothing-to-do position on a bale of hay, nonetheless—told her to stop.

Sweating, huffing, and undoubtedly red-faced, she dragged herself over to where he was lazing in the shade, looking perfectly fresh, clean, and effortlessly handsome. As usual his expression gave nothing away, but his blue eyes were suspiciously bright—as if he were holding in laughter.

Her eyes narrowed. "Don't you need to 'warm

up' as well?"

"I was up early with some of your brother's men scouting Ben Vorlich."

"You mean you've been climbing mountains all morning and look like…?"

He grinned. "Like what?"

"Nothing," she grumbled, slamming her mouth shut. He knew perfectly well how he looked.

"And I was running," he corrected. "Not climbing. I need to get stronger, too."

Unconsciously, her eyes dropped to his arms and chest, taking in every inch of that strength. He didn't look as if he needed any more.

She flushed when she realized what he'd done— tricked her into looking at his body—and quickly lifted her gaze back to his face, where admittedly it wasn't much safer.

Angry at herself for falling for his ploy, she snapped, "Are we going to get to work then?"

He stood and bowed with an exaggerated flourish. "I'm at your command, my lady."

But unfortunately, for the next few hours it was the opposite, and she was at *his* command while he barked out instructions.

"Come at me again," he said for the third time. "You are still hesitating. You want to be quick and purposeful and take advantage of the element of surprise. This isn't about you facing off with an opponent in a knife fight. It's about you using your knife to take advantage of an opening to escape or to kill someone who is threatening you." His expression was graver and more serious than it had been all week. His eyes bored into her as he scanned her face. "You understand what we are doing here, don't you, Annie? If you pull a weapon, you have to be ready to use it. Your aim is to inflict as much damage as you can with one strike. You may only get one chance, so you need to make it count. If you can't do that, we are wasting our time."

The tinge of disappointment in his voice made something in her chest pinch. "I'm trying, but…"

"But what?"

"I don't want to hurt you."

He grinned.

Misunderstanding, she bristled. "Why are you smiling? Is it so hard to conceive that I could put a nick in that steely armor of yours?"

His grin deepened. "Not at all. That's the goal. When you can stick me with that blade, I'll know I've done my job."

Highland warriors were strange creatures. "So, you want me to hurt you?"

He nodded.

She smiled sweetly. "Then shouldn't we be using a steel blade? I will be able to do a lot more damage."

He laughed. "Nice try, killer. We'll switch to a real blade when I'm assured that you aren't going to accidentally cut your finger off."

She lunged at him again—this time with purpose—hoping to catch him unprepared. But there was something she was learning about Niall. He was always prepared and ready for the attack, even when it seemed as if he was not paying attention. There was a watchfulness to him that hadn't been there before. She supposed it had come from all the months he'd spent on the run being hunted by the Campbells.

She felt a twinge in her chest that might have been worry and pushed it aside. *One month or one year,* she reminded herself, but blast it, it had only been six days! Being with Niall had always been so easy. So much had changed, but that hadn't.

Niall blocked her attack with ease. Sliding to the side, he grabbed the hand that held the blade and twisted her arm around her back until she was pinned up against him.

The contact caused her to freeze, and the knife fell from her hand.

NIALL SWORE INWARDLY. HIS MOVEMENTS HAD been instinctive. When he'd seen the knife coming at him, he'd simply reacted.

She's surprised him—and not for the first time, although he'd never tell her that. He didn't want his praise to go to her head and for her to become overconfident.

The idea of her ever pulling a knife on someone still filled him with a sickly, almost vomit-inducing dread. But he had to admit that she wasn't without some natural ability. Who would have thought that a lass could learn to fight? He'd offered to instruct her solely as a means to an end. His own end. To earn her forgiveness. He hadn't expected to take it seriously.

He'd dismissed Patrick's comments about her skill as brotherly bias and exaggeration. Of course, Niall knew from some of their childhood tussling and playing around that, like her brothers, Annie was unnaturally strong for her size.

But she was still a *lass*—and a relatively small one at that. After what had happened to her, she was even more delicate in appearance now. Whatever soft childhood roundness she'd once had was gone. She was too thin—which made her strength all the more unexpected. But that would serve her well if—God forbid—she ever needed to fight. It was an advantage to be underestimated by your opponent.

Although she lacked the quickness and experience that came from years of practice, her instincts were good, as she'd just proved. Now she was pressed against his chest, and he was breathing in the dangerous mix of sunshine and the lavender soap in her silky, dark hair.

He'd been trying to be patient. Keeping his distance and not wanting to push her into something that she might not be ready for. Like this type of closeness where their bodies were touching, and he could feel every one of the sweet curves he'd been trying not to notice the past six days in full, mouthwatering relief.

Jesus.

Awareness hit him hard, sinking through him like a weight. His senses were drugged by the feel, the scent, the sound of her hitched breathing. He could practically taste her on his lips. The memory of the one kiss they'd shared came back to him in a hot and heavy rush.

It made his knees weaken and his resolve flounder.

He would have found the strength to resist the fierce pull coming over him if he thought she might be scared. But she wasn't. She was stunned maybe, but not scared or in any way panicked.

She looked up at him, her eyes swimming in confusion, her lips parted in innocent invitation, and damn it, that was more than he could take. He loved her so much, and for two years he'd dreamed of being in this position again, except this time he would do it right.

He let go her arm, which he hadn't been holding very tightly, lowered his head, and covered her mouth with his.

At the first taste of her, he groaned. The warm-honey sweetness engulfed him with hunger and yearning. His memories hadn't been exaggerated. This was… she was… *perfect*.

For one precious instant, he felt her soften. Felt her succumb to the passion that had sprung up between them so instantly the last time.

But maybe he was too overeager. Too optimistic. Maybe he foolishly thought that he could rectify everything that had happened between them with a kiss.

Whatever it was, he'd erred and moved too fast. His attempt to fold her in his arms and deepen the kiss caused the very thing he'd been trying to avoid.

She pushed him away. "Stop!" She stared up at him in fury, clenching her fists. "What do you think you are doing?"

It was pretty obvious what he was doing, but he knew she didn't just mean the kiss. He'd buggered up. Again.

But thank God, it was anger shooting back at him in her eyes and not fear. He would have stuck himself with that damned wooden knife that she kept complaining about if he thought he'd frightened her.

"I'm sorry," he said, dragging his fingers back through his hair, which had slipped forward when he'd kissed her. "I didn't mean for that to happen. The last thing I want to do is rush you."

"Rush me?" Outrage turned on him. "Is that what you think is going on here? Are you just biding your time until I succumb to the great, irresistible charms of Niall Lamont? Have you heard nothing I've said?"

Now she wasn't the only one who was angry. Niall's pent-up frustration caught up with him in one fell swoop. "I've heard every word you've said. For two bloody years I've been waiting to hear you talk to me again. Do you think I'd miss any of it? But I should have known that you would be needlessly stubborn. You've been that way for as long as I've known you, and whatever else has changed, that sure as Hades hasn't."

She flushed and straightened her spine as if she could span the nearly twelve inches that separated their heights. "Needlessly? What do you mean by that? Do you think I don't know my own mind? And if my faults bother you so much, why are you here?"

"I didn't say it was a fault," although it was sure as hell bothering him right now. "I said it was who you are. Like your brothers and most of your clansmen, you are stubborn, tenacious, tough, and loyal. You are a fighter and a survivor even when the odds are against you. You are every inch a Mac-Gregor, and that's why I'm here. Because I know that, no matter how much I hurt you or what hell you suffered at those bastards' hands, you are too damned stubborn to quit. I know that the girl who gave me her heart is too loyal to take it away no matter how much of an arse I've been or whether I deserve it or not."

He lowered his voice, realizing he didn't need to shout anymore. She was definitely listening, hanging on every word, as a matter of fact. She blinked up at him, and he didn't think it was the sun in her eyes that was making them shiny. For the first time, it seemed he'd penetrated the iron shield that she'd erected around her heart.

"I know the woman who has been out here practicing the same drills over and over for days with a wooden knife is tenacious and isn't going to give up no matter how hard I try to bore her to death."

He probably should have quit while he was ahead and not added that last part. The burgeoning emotion in her eyes was a lot harder to see through her suddenly narrowed gaze.

"God's teeth, I should have known something was going on! Did you and my brother come up with this together, or was it your brilliant idea to train me at such a snail's pace?"

"Your brother didn't have anything to do with it. But I wouldn't really call it an 'idea.'"

Forgetting that she'd just pushed him away a few moments before, she came right up to him, toe-to-toe. "Oh yeah, then what would you call it?"

He winced a little sheepishly. "Being careful?"

Her eyes were so narrow now they'd turned into two sharp points. "And the running this morning. Was that 'careful,' too?"

He made another face and had to fight hard not to laugh. But some things never changed; he loved seeing her riled up. "I believe you said something about me running once?"

He didn't think he'd ever seen her get so mad. She looked as if she were trying to think of the most painful ways to kill him. He was glad that wooden knife was still lying on the ground. Ever so slyly, he moved his heel to stand on the handle and felt a crack.

"You are a despot of the worst kind, Niall Lamont. What kind of man takes his petty grievances out on a woman under his control?"

He laughed aloud at that one. They both knew how ridiculous that characterization was. Annie MacGregor would never let any man control her. God pity the poor fool who tried.

"Oh no. You don't get to play the 'weaker vessel' when you want to, love. Not when I'm teaching you how to stick me with a knife. And two years is a long time to make me wait for being an idiot. But just because I took a little pleasure in it doesn't make anything I asked you to do not important. Running *will* make you stronger and improve your endurance."

She looked marginally—marginally—mollified. "Well, at least we agree on one thing."

"What's that?"

"That you are an idiot."

"*Was*," he corrected. "*Was* an idiot. I should have gotten down on my knee after that kiss at Dunvegan and asked you to marry me."

"So now that you can no longer be chief, I'm good enough for you?"

All jesting fell by the wayside. He was very sober when he responded. "I never wanted to be chief, Annie. That position belonged to Malcolm, and now it belongs to Brian. But you were always good enough for me, and I'm sorry if I ever made you feel differently. I thought I was doing my duty. I was the second son; an important alliance through marriage to secure my future and better our clan was expected. I knew my father was trying to arrange an alliance with a Gordon heiress, and I thought it was my duty to go along with it. But I forgot something important."

"What?" She was doing her best to make it seem as if the answer wasn't important to her, but he could sense it was.

"I forgot how much my father adored my mother. He would have understood if I'd told him I loved you and wanted to marry you." He took a chance and reached down to cup her small chin in his fingers. He didn't want her to be able to look away. He wanted her to know he meant every word he said. "What we had was special, and I should have known that—especially after that kiss."

His words seemed to be penetrating until he said the word kiss. A shadow cast over her gaze before it shuttered completely.

She shook off his hold and stepped back. "It won't work, Niall. No matter what you say. What we had is gone, and it can't be put back by pretty words and apologies."

His frustration got the better of him. "Why the hell can't it? The way I see it, the only thing standing in the way is your damned pride."

She flushed. "Well, you don't see everything."

She was just being ornery now, and Niall's cool slipped a little further. "So why don't you tell me what I'm supposedly missing?"

As he'd never seen her twisting her hands so anxiously before, it took him a moment to realize that she wasn't angry anymore but upset. "I don't feel like that anymore, all right? Don't you see? I don't want… I can't…"

She stopped, tears filling her eyes.

Niall stilled. Suddenly he did see. The burning ache in his chest was only outweighed by the stabbing in his gut.

If Colin Campbell or any of those bastards were standing before him right now, he'd tear them apart with his bare hands. Limb by bloody limb.

"You don't want me anymore?"

Just saying the words hurt. It hurt in a way he'd never imagined. In his chest. In his heart. In his soul. She'd cut him apart and left him in pieces.

She shook her head. "I'm sorry, Niall."

And before he could stop her, she turned and fled across the *barmkin* toward the castle.

He didn't go after her. He slid to the ground and put his head in his hands, stunned by the unexpected blow and wondering at the unimaginable hell that she must have gone through to make her lose something that had been such a vital part of her. Her passion. Her passion *for him*.

Jesus.

For the first time in his life, Niall wondered if there was a hurdle in front of him that might be too high to jump over.

𝒞

HE BELIEVED HER NOW.

One look at Niall's devastated face and Annie knew he understood the truth. She didn't want him anymore. She didn't any man after what those horrible men had done to her.

But if she thought she would get some kind of satisfaction from hurting him like that—hurting him in the same way he'd hurt her—she was wrong. Apparently, she was less coldhearted than she thought. Hurting him hadn't made her feel any better; it made her feel worse.

A lot worse.

She'd just wanted him to understand that she meant what she said about it being over. Now he did.

If only she could stop picturing his face. She might as well have taken a sword and cut him off at the knees. The effect would have been the same. His face had drained. The brash confidence and warrior's arrogance of a man who had always been admired by men and women alike was stripped away. He'd looked shattered. Destroyed. As if she'd just knocked down the very foundation that he'd been standing on.

It was what she wanted, wasn't it? For him to leave her alone, to move on the way that she had.

Then why did she feel so… awful? Almost ill. As if her stomach had been tied in thousands of knots and was being pulled in multiple directions.

She half expected to see him ride out of the castle gate and never look back. If she looked out the window in her tower room more than a few—

dozen—times that day, that was why.

She wondered if she might have missed his departure when he didn't appear for the midday meal, but when her brother caught her staring at the place that Niall usually occupied at the table among her brother's guardsmen, he not very casually mentioned that Niall had gone to town on an errand.

The nearest town, Balquhidder, was about seven miles away, so she assumed he wouldn't be gone long. She refrained from asking why, although her curiosity was killing her.

Patrick clearly suspected her interest, but his infuriating smile suggested that he'd make her ask before telling her.

She gritted her teeth. *Brothers!*

She tried the usual things to keep herself busy— reading a book, working in the garden, helping with baby Iain—but her mind kept drifting back to that morning.

Something was niggling at her, but she couldn't quite put her finger on what. Somehow—probably not by mistake—she found herself sitting next to Alys while the baby napped in the antechamber of Lizzie and Patrick's solar. Her sister by marriage was in the kitchens going over the weekly menu with the cook.

They sat in silence for a while before Alys ventured, "Is something troubling you, lass? You seem distracted."

The maidservant's knowing gaze shot to the embroidery Annie was supposed to be working on that sat untouched in her lap.

Annie flushed and nodded.

"Did something happen with Niall? I know you've been training with him for the past week."

Six days—not that she was counting. Tomorrow would be day number seven. The week was over, and she could tell him to leave. Which was exactly what she should do despite how much she liked training with him. Not just training. She liked being with him again. She'd forgotten how much.

Before he came, everything had been fine. She'd known her mind. But he was confusing her.

"He kissed me," she blurted, embarrassed.

Alys held her gaze, obviously trying to gauge Annie's feelings on the matter. "And you didn't want him to kiss you?"

Annie shook her head furiously.

"Did it frighten you?"

She thought for a minute. Surprisingly, it hadn't. "No."

"Then you did not like it?"

Annie frowned and bit her lip. She had thought that she wouldn't. Which wasn't actually the same as not liking it. "It was… nice."

Until he'd tried to deepen the kiss and she'd frozen.

Alys gave her a wry smile. "Then I don't understand the problem?"

"It wasn't the same." Alys frowned, and Annie tried to explain. "The first time we kissed a couple of years ago, I felt such…" She struggled to say the embarrassing word.

"Passion?" Alys filled in.

Annie nodded again, grateful that she'd come up with a better word than lust. But lust was exactly how she used to feel. As shameful as it was to admit.

Ladies weren't supposed to feel things like that. At least that's what the church said. But her *passion* had never felt like a sin with Niall.

It had felt like heaven. A very hot heaven.

"I would say that was normal after what you went through. You just need to give yourself some time. Those feelings will come back."

Annie's distress returned. "You don't understand. With Niall… it never used to be like that. I used to look at him and practically want to tear his clothes off. Now the idea of it repulses me." She knew what lay underneath those clothes, and what had hurt her. "What if I can never be normal again?" she finished in a whisper.

The older woman reached down and took Annie's chin, tilting her face back to hers. "You will feel that way again," she said firmly. "With the man you love. Trust me, I know. I felt the same way as you, although I was not a maid and already knew the pleasures of the marriage bed. The first few times after…" She shuddered. "I thought Donnan would find out. He knew something was wrong. I could not respond in the way I had before. But he loved me and was patient with what he thought was a sudden onslaught of maidenly modesty." She shook her head, her eyes filling with the memory. "Do you know that fool man thought it was something he'd done? It broke my heart to see him so upset. I think that forced me out of my cocoon. I couldn't stand to see him take the blame for something that he hadn't done. If your Niall loves you as much as I think he does, he will grant you that same patience and understanding." She paused for a moment, looking deeper into Annie's thoughts than she wanted her to. "That is *if* you still love him?"

Annie wanted to look away. Wanted to hide her feelings from even herself. But the squeezing in her chest didn't lie. "I don't know. I shouldn't."

And despite Alys's certainty, Annie wasn't sure she would ever feel the same way again. Would that be fair to Niall? A wife who couldn't bear his touch?

She had much to think on. She thanked Alys and stood to return to her room. But before she closed the door behind her, she turned. "I do think you are wrong about one thing."

"What's that?" Alys said.

"I understand why you didn't say anything at the time, but I don't think your husband would have loved you any less had you told him what happened. Not if he loved you then half as much as he does today."

CHAPTER SIX

❦

NIALL WAS MORE RELIEVED THAN he wanted to admit when he saw Annie heading toward him the next morning wearing her training clothes. He was keenly aware of what day it was and wasn't sure after what had happened yesterday whether she would just send him on his way. Well, if she was planning to, at least he had until after practice to change her mind.

He also had a secret weapon if necessary—literally.

She greeted him with a nod. "You are here early. I'd hoped to get some target practice in first."

Niall didn't comment. Tossing a knife at some straw with painted targets might not be practical in an attack, but it was a fun pastime among warriors.

The thought took him aback. Was that what she was? A warrior? He would have laughed at the notion a few weeks ago. But now the idea didn't seem so far-fetched. The lass had some skill and as much determination as any of the young warriors he'd trained. Maybe more.

"What's your record?" Niall asked.

Annie knew exactly what he meant. "I've hit the

center three times in a row twice."

"From how far out?"

"Ten paces."

"That's pretty good."

Her mouth quirked into a small smile. "Is that actually a compliment?"

He returned her smile. "No. Merely an observation."

That elicited an eye roll. "I should have known better. What do I have to do to get a compliment from you?"

"Make it ten times in a row, and I'll think about it."

She gave a sharp sound of disgust. "It will take me years to master that kind of skill."

"I did it in one year when I started out training."

She gave him a hard look, her eyes narrowed as if not sure whether to believe him. "Then I will do it in six months."

He chuckled. That brazen confidence was so typically the Annie he used to know that he couldn't help responding in kind. "I hope you don't like sleeping, because you'll need every hour in the day to even have a shot at fulfilling that boast."

"We'll see," she said, apparently unconcerned. "But to answer your question, no, I don't—not anymore."

It took him a moment to realize that she meant sleeping, and he instantly sobered. He bit back a curse. "I'm sorry. I wasn't thinking." He raked his fingers back through his hair. "I seem to be doing that a lot of late. You have nightmares?"

Of course, she did. *He* had nightmares, damn it, and he hadn't lived it.

She nodded and looked away.

"Do you want to talk about it?"

Her head spun back toward him in disbelief. "With you?" She looked as incredulous as she sounded, but at least she was meeting his gaze again. "I don't think so."

"Why not?" Niall wasn't completely sure he wanted to hear the details, but he wanted her to know that she could confide in him.

Her cheeks flushed and her eyes blazed with fury. "Because I don't want to talk about it, all right? I *never* want to talk about it! Don't you understand?"

Her pain was killing him. Niall wanted nothing more than to take her in his arms and comfort her, but he had to remind himself that what he wanted and what she needed might be different things now. He also recalled the disaster of the day before when he'd kissed her. "No, I don't," he said quietly. "But I'm trying to. If you'll let me."

His response only seemed to increase her frustration. "Why are you being like this? Did you forget what I told you yesterday? I don't feel anything. Nothing, all right?"

It wasn't all right. None of this was all right. "I didn't forget, and if you never want me to kiss or touch you again, I will accept that. But it doesn't change how I feel about you or that I want you to be my wife."

ANNIE WAS STUNNED INTO SILENCE. SHE GAPED at him incredulously. "So what are you suggesting? That I will be your wife, and you will take other women to bed?"

The change that came over Niall was instantaneous. His back went as stiff as a pike and his expression turned granite cold. Especially his eyes. They could freeze the loch in summer.

He was clearly affronted—as if she'd just impugned his honor in the worst way. "If that is what you think of me, then maybe I am wasting my time here."

She felt a tug in her heart that felt suspiciously like a twinge of panic. She didn't care whether he stayed... did she?

Maybe more than she wanted to admit, because she found herself explaining. "What am I supposed to think? That you will live the life of a monk? I know it's something I'm supposed to pretend to not know about, but many men have mistresses."

He gave her a hard, unyielding stare of challenge—laden with a heavy dose of disappointment. "Does your brother? Did your father? Do any of the men you know who profess to love their wives have mistresses?"

She looked down, properly shamed. Patrick would die before hurting Lizzie like that, and from everything she knew about her father, he'd adored her mother. "I don't know. I guess not."

"I would never dishonor you like that, and as I've been living 'like a monk' for well over a year now, I guess you could say I'm used to it."

It took her a moment to process what he'd said. She looked back up to meet his gaze. She couldn't hide her incredulity. "You have?"

He nodded. "You are the only woman I want in my bed, Annie. And if you do not wish to be there, no one else will take your place."

She didn't know what to say—or how to say it. "But…"

When she didn't finish, he prodded, "But what?"

Her cheeks were burning. This wasn't exactly a topic she was used to discussing. "But what about your needs?"

She thought his mouth twitched with amusement, but his voice was deadly serious. "There are other ways of satisfying my 'needs.'"

She wouldn't ask. Even though she wanted to. She really wanted to. "But men have urges that they can't control."

He frowned. "Who told you that nonsense?"

She chewed on her lip uncomfortably. "I don't know. I've just heard… Everyone knows that."

"What you've heard is wrong. Dead wrong. I assure you any urges I have can be controlled. I wanted you more than any woman I've ever wanted in my life, and I resisted your many very blatant and sometimes overt invitations for two years, didn't I?" She scanned his face intently, clearly wanting to believe him. He reached down to gently cup her chin in his hand. "Not all men are lust-raged rapists, Annie. What those men did to you is not normal. No matter how much I wanted you, no matter how enflamed my body, I would always stop if you wanted me to. Always."

"Even when… even in the midst…"

"Always," he said in a voice that brokered no room for doubt.

He sounded as if he believed what he said. But did she? She didn't know. There was one way to find out, but she wasn't sure she was ready for that.

Although the thought of it didn't frighten her as much as she expected. Actually, it didn't frighten her at all. What would it have been like if the first time she'd experienced the act it had been in love and not violence? Would it have felt so repugnant? So disgusting? So awful?

That was one more thing those men had taken from her. Not her maidenhead, but the chance to have her first time be with someone she loved. Someone whose touch she'd once craved.

He seemed to read her mind. His thumb stroked the skin of her jaw with as much tenderness as was in his voice. His hand was warm, and it seemed to flow through her. Not in the frantic way it used to before, but in a slower, deeper, more powerful way.

"When you are ready—if you are ready—I will prove it to you."

This time curiosity got the better of her and she asked, "How?"

His mouth curved enigmatically. "There are ways that you can be in control."

Her in control? How? Now it wasn't just her curiosity, but her mind was racing in all kinds of directions.

Probably knowing exactly how much he'd roused her curiosity, he turned the conversation before she could ask specifics. "We should get started if you want to practice today. I agreed to ride out with your brother later this morning."

Annie frowned. "Is something wrong?"

Niall shook his head. "He asked for my advice on some land he is thinking about purchasing from the Laird of Ardvorlich for grazing sheep."

It was strange to think of it now as so much had

changed, but at one time Niall had been the quint-
essential Highland laird, focused on increasing the
profitability of his father's lands in Cowal and Bute
through farming and grazing. Malcolm might have
been the designated chief and the man who would
lead the clan into battle, but it was Niall's ambition
and financial acumen that would have taken the
clan into the future. That same ambition was what
had made him think he couldn't marry her.

What would he do now that that the role of a
laird had been blocked to him?

Before she could ask, he slipped something out
of his belt and put it behind his back. "I have something for you, but before we continue, I want you
to agree to something."

She knew him too well, which meant she knew
when he was up to no good. She eyed him suspiciously. "What?"

"Another week."

Before she could reply, he proved that her suspicion was well-warranted by revealing what he'd
been hiding behind his back.

She sucked in her breath, the gleam of metal
shimmering like a jewel in the morning sunlight
in his hand.

She met his trying-not-to-laugh gaze.

"You are an evil man Niall Lamont."

He didn't bother to deny it and lowered the
small knife that he'd been dangling like an apple
from a tree right in front of her eyes. Suddenly she
understood Eve's temptation. "Then you do not
want it?"

She snatched it from his hand before he could
slide it back in the scabbard. "You know very well

that I do." She turned the knife in her hand, the handle fitting perfectly. It was as if it had been made for her. Suddenly she realized that it had. "You had it made for me. That was where you went yesterday."

It wasn't a question, so he didn't need to respond. She felt something in her chest squeeze hard. If he'd wanted to find a way back into her heart, he would have been hard-pressed to find a more perfect gift. As he no doubt well knew.

Niall Lamont did still know her better than anyone in the world. That hadn't changed after all.

CHAPTER SEVEN

NIALL GOT HIS WEEK. AND over the next few days, he felt as if he'd gotten far more. He was earning Annie's trust again. He could feel that formidable will dissolving. That steely barrier she'd erected around her heart eroding.

He was winning her back, and it took everything he had not to try to race to the finish line. But her words a few days ago had chilled him. He knew that in the world they lived in men's base urges were often given free rein and excused as nature. Rape as a weapon of war was a manifestation of that belief.

But that wasn't him, and it wasn't all men. He needed to show her that.

Annie had experienced violence, force, and lust. He wasn't going to do anything to create confusion in her mind about him, his level of control, or his intentions.

Even if it killed him.

And there had been plenty of times in the past few days that it nearly had. She'd relaxed, which meant that when they were training, she didn't so obviously attempt to avoid any kind of bodily contact with him. Once or twice, he thought she might have even gone out of her way to instigate and prolong the contact that did occur.

Yesterday, when he'd been teaching her a foot-work maneuver to put her opponent on the ground, she'd fallen on top of him. When she'd slowly worked her way up his body to sitting astride him, his blood was pounding so hard and hot he thought it would burst from his veins.

No matter how many thoughts of cold dunks in the loch or naked old nuns that he tried to picture, he hadn't been able to control the blood rush to one part of his body. And he was too big a man to hide behind the leather of his jerkin and trews.

She'd pretended not to feel his erection, but it had been too prominent to miss. The fact that she didn't move or attempt to shift her weight from that very throbbing part of him made the throb-bing all that much worse.

He'd controlled his needs all right. With a very cold bath and a very firm grip of his hand later that night.

She might not want him the same way she once had, but she didn't *not* want him either. He just had to give her time. Unfortunately, he didn't know how much time he had left.

He'd ridden out with Patrick the other day not just to look at the land, as he'd told her, but also because they'd heard rumors of the king's men in the area, and Niall wanted to get word to his clansmen who were waiting nearby. He had them hunting for his pursuers right now to try to send them in the wrong direction.

Niall needed to tell Annie his plans, but he sensed

that she wasn't ready yet, and he didn't want to force a decision on her before she needed to make one. But that day was fast approaching. He could feel the urgency in the cold air of the Michaelmas season upon them.

Niall thought that he'd done a good job of containing the knowledge of his identity to a select handful of Patrick's guardsmen and immediate family until the end of the second week of training when he learned differently—while simultaneously ensuring that his presence would not remain a secret for long.

There was a small group of Campbell guardsmen whom Niall usually tried to avoid. The men were part of the contingent that Jamie Campbell had insisted upon at the castle when his sister married Patrick. Niall understood that their captain, Donnan, whom Patrick trusted, had been informed of his true identity, but the rest of the Campbells had been told that he was a "Murray" (aka MacGregor) clansman. But as Niall's resemblance to his sister, Caitrina—their new lady—was marked, he thought it better not to draw too much attention to himself.

There was one Campbell guardsman in particular whom Niall didn't like the looks of. Or rather, more precisely, he didn't like the way the young guardsman looked at Annie. More than once, Niall had caught him staring at her for too long—too intently—and then whispering something in one of his compatriots' ears, which inevitably caused smirks and laughter. It made Niall's hackles rise. He didn't need to know what the other man was saying to know that he wouldn't like it.

He found out just how much he didn't like it on the evening of a feast that was being held to celebrate the wedding of one of Patrick's guardsmen. Niall arrived late after he and Robbie MacGregor—who'd returned from his errand at Molach—had sparred longer than they intended. It turned out the young guardsman was nearly his equal with a long sword, and the chance to have real competition had proved invigorating. The fact that they were in love with the same woman might have given their sparring an added edge, but Robbie seemed to accept Niall's presence with a stoic good grace that made it hard not to like him.

With most of the tables full by the time they arrived, Niall and Robbie took a seat in the back of the room behind a table of boisterous Campbell guardsmen. From the sounds of it, the *cuirm* and ale had obviously been flowing for some time.

Niall was seated almost directly behind the young guardsman he didn't like—Connell, he'd heard him called—when Annie rushed past them. She was obviously late, too, as her dark hair, which hung loosely down her back from under her simple linen coif, fell in damp waves down her back. Her cheeks were flushed as if she'd just stepped from her bath, and the plush velvet crimson gown she was wearing clung to her form as if slightly damp.

She looked mouthwateringly beautiful, and Niall's wasn't the only gaze that followed her form down the aisle.

"Usually I don't like other men's leavings," he heard a voice behind him say. "But in her case, I'll make an exception. If the lass needs more sword practice after the outlaw is done with her, I'll be happy to give her a few more lessons—especially in oiling. I'd like to have that mouth polishing my steel."

Niall recognized the voice right away. The fact that the other man was slurring didn't penetrate the red haze of rage that descended over him, nor did the fact that Niall was only one against a table of at least a dozen.

He stood, turned, picked the man up by the back of his neck to face him, and slammed his fist into his jaw. Connell went flying backward and landed on the table, sending food and drink scattering with a crash. The curses and gasps of surprise were followed by the sound of benches falling back and hitting the floor as men jumped to their feet. Niall soon found himself in the center of a melee, being pummeled from all directions by Connell's furious—and drunk—friends.

He wasn't alone though. Robbie was standing beside him. But even with two, the numbers weren't in their favor. Niall lost track of Robbie as he landed on the floor and boots were added to the fists that were striking most of his body.

He heard a crack and knew from the pain in his side there had to be at least one broken rib.

Another particularly powerful blow to the head made him see stars. He might have lost consciousness for a moment, because when he came to, the men had been pulled off him and Patrick MacGregor was pulling him to his feet.

"What the hell is the meaning of this?" Annie's brother demanded. "Connell said you attacked him for no reason."

"That isn't true," said a voice from Niall's side.

Niall looked over and was relieved to see Robbie standing beside him and, except for a bloody lip and cheek, looking relatively unscathed.

Patrick gazed back and forth between them and the Campbells. Niall was glad to see that Connell had to be propped up by two of his friends and looked considerably worse than even Niall felt.

"Who is going to tell me what happened?"

Niall exchanged a glance with Robbie, who understood, and then he scanned the Campbell faces, who from their grim expressions also seemed to understand. Connell Campbell's skin had turned the grayish tone of a man who knew and feared what could be coming his way.

If Niall repeated what he'd said, Patrick would continue where Niall and Robbie had left off— and this time he wouldn't have his friends to rescue him.

But Niall wasn't going to repeat what he said. He would never repeat the crude words that would only make Annie the subject of more gossip and speculation.

Niall had been too happy and grateful to spend time with her to think how it would look. He'd thought they were out of the way enough not to draw attention. Apparently, he was wrong.

Niall's jaw flexed intractably. His teeth practically gritted together as he said, "It was nothing."

He could practically feel the collective sigh of relief that came from the Campbells.

Donnan had come up to stand beside his new chieftain. "Is that true?" he demanded of the Campbell clansmen.

One of the older guardsmen nodded. "Aye, it was a misunderstanding. Too much drink," he added.

Patrick's steely-eyed gaze didn't leave Niall's face. He didn't believe a word of it. But he'd probably guessed what had happened.

Niall looked around, relieved to see that Annie wasn't part of the crowd watching them. Neither was Elizabeth Campbell or the other ladies from the dais. Patrick must have sent them from the room when the fighting broke out.

"I see," Patrick said. It was clear he did. "Well, the party is over. I will decide your punishment for breaking the peace tomorrow."

The men started to disperse. Niall went to follow Robbie, but Patrick stopped him. "Not you. I want to talk to you."

Niall sighed. He should have known it wouldn't be that easy. He followed Patrick out of the great hall and down the corridor to his private solar.

Patrick motioned to a chair, which Niall gratefully slid into. He was pretty beat up, and he was shamefully close to swaying.

"What happened?"

"I told you."

"Don't give me that shite, Niall. I want to know what he said."

Niall met his anger head-on. "No, you don't."

Patrick swore. He sat down in a chair behind his desk, looking a little beat up himself. "I hoped to spare Annie from gossip by bringing her here."

Niall suspected that was an exercise in futility. Gossip would always follow her. That was one of the reasons he hoped she would see the value in what he intended to propose to her. "It's probably my fault. I didn't realize the attention our practice was gathering."

Both men sat in silence. Their shared pain for the woman they both loved was palpable.

"I would spare her all this if I could," Niall said.

"But you can't," Patrick said glumly. "And neither can I."

It was a horrible acknowledgment for them both. Helplessness was not a state familiar to a Highland warrior.

"Go," Patrick said after a minute. "See to your wounds. Your face looks like hell, and from the way you are holding your side, I'm guessing you have a few broken ribs that should be tended to. The healer has a storeroom next to the ale house where she has set up a small infirmary and apothecary. You should find her there."

Which made sense as Niall knew the healer was also the castle's alewife. Not all castles had buildings for brewing beer, but Niall knew that Patrick sold it to other local lairds as an extra source of income.

Niall nodded. "I should warn you that there might be other problems."

"What kind of problems?"

"Some of the Campbell soldiers seem to know who I am."

Patrick's curse echoed Niall's thoughts. "I'll talk to Donnan to keep them quiet. But you look so much like your sister it was bound to come out."

"I don't want to bring you trouble."

Patrick gave a sharp scoff. "Then you shouldn't have come here. But if you can make my sister happy, I might not kill you for it."

As Niall suspected that was the best deal he was

likely to get, he left.

Could he make Annie happy? He would do everything in his power to try.

ANNIE HAD BEEN CLIMBING THE WALLS SINCE HER brother had sent the women from the great hall after the fighting broke out. Fighting in which Niall was at the center! She'd caught one quick glimpse of him before he'd disappeared into the mob of Campbells and Alys's husband had steered the ladies from the room.

Lizzie, Alys, and Annie had waited in the keep for Patrick to return. Although he'd assured them everything was all right and that it was a misunderstanding, Annie's heart dropped when she asked about Niall and learned he was "fine" and had been sent to the healer.

Clearly, she and her brother had very different definitions of fine! She raced across the *barmkin* and burst into the storeroom right as Niall was lifting off his shirt.

Both the healer and Niall turned to her as she entered.

The shock of awareness akin to running into a stone wall at the sight of his chest turned to a cry of horror when she saw his face.

Their eyes met. "I'm fine. It looks worse than it is."

Annie doubted that—and apparently, he shared her brother's same flawed ideal of "fine." Blood, cuts, and bruises were most certainly *not* fine!

She looked to the healer, whose cackle of amusement seemed to fit her appearance. Not all healers were old women who conjured thoughts of black cauldrons and witchcraft, although this one was. But her clear blue eyes were kind. "Aye, don't you worry, lassie. Your braw lad will be bonny again soon enough."

Annie didn't protest her erroneous take on the situation but stood by the door while the woman continued her ministrations. While the healer examined Niall's ribs and back, Annie did the same.

Good gracious! She swallowed—hard. She'd seen Niall without his shirt a number of times when he was younger. He and Iain used to love to race each other across Loch Katrine, and Annie used to serve as judge on the winner when it was close, as it inevitably was.

But the broad span of heavily muscled chest and arms that was before her now looked nothing like the one she remembered. He'd added at least a few stone worth of granite-hard, expertly sculpted muscle. She'd never realized that muscles could be that sharply defined. There didn't seem to be an ounce of extra flesh anywhere that she could see.

She moved a few steps to the right to get a better look at his stomach just to be sure. But good Lord, that was even more defined! The laundress could beat the clothes against all the ridges and lines of muscle working their way up his stomach.

Something strange started to happen. Annie's heart started to beat a little faster—and heavier—but her breathing slowed. She felt flushed and hot—as if she'd just walked into the bakehouse instead of the infirmary.

But the moment she realized she was experiencing awareness again, it fled when he flinched as the healer inspected his ribs and Annie saw the mottled red bruise on his other side.

She must have made a sound because he looked at her again. "It's a few cracked ribs, Annie. Nothing I haven't experienced before."

"I'll be the judge of that," the healer said. "Take a deep breath. Does it hurt?"

"No," he answered too quickly. The healer stared at him until he relented. "Not badly," he amended.

She made a sound of disgust and continued her examination. "There doesn't look to be too much bleeding and your lungs sound clear. I'll put some salve on your side and your lass can help me with the wrapping."

Annie wasn't sure she wanted to go anywhere near all that bare skin and raw masculine energy, but she tentatively stepped forward to help. She was careful not to touch him, and in about ten minutes his ribs were bound in a sheet of linen and his wounds were washed and tended.

He did look considerably better, but she suspected he would be turning various hues of black and blue in the next few hours.

"I'll make a posset for you to drink later," the healer said. "Your lass can help you with your shirt."

Before Annie could stop her, the old woman turned and left the room, closing the door behind her.

The room suddenly seemed about ten times smaller, darker, and warmer.

Annie felt as if her feet were stuck in a bog. She couldn't move. Her body was too heavy.

From his seat on the stool in front her, Niall

watched her with the dark, predatory intensity of a hawk. Nothing was escaping that steely-eyed gaze.

She flushed, her cheeks growing even hotter, and had to resist the urge not to fan herself with her hand. He was sitting too close. Crowding her. It wouldn't take more than a nudge for him to reach out and pull her onto his lap.

"You feel it, don't you?"

She wanted to lie. Wanted to turn away from that piercing gaze and shake her head. But she couldn't. She felt it all right. It was wrapping around her in a sultry embrace, but she didn't know whether to give in to it or run away in terror. She felt like doing both.

She nodded tentatively.

"Don't be scared, sweetheart. I told you that I would never hurt you." He paused. "You can touch me if you want."

She shook her head. "You're hurt."

"Not that hurt. And believe me, your touch will only make me feel better—a hell of a lot better."

Annie was too curious to argue. The ache to put her hands on the wide spans of tanned skin too tempting. "But what if…? You won't…?"

"You are in control, Annie. I will not touch you unless you want me to."

Annie eyed him warily, but eventually her curiosity overrode whatever hesitation she might have.

She took a step closer to him so that she was standing between his legs. His head was a little below her eye level, which made him seem not so threatening.

Which was laughable as pretty much everything about Niall Lamont was threatening and overpowering. Particularly his body.

Tentatively, she reached out with her right hand to rest it on the hard rock of his shoulder. She gasped at the contact, at the sensation of all that warm bare skin under her fingers, and at the blast of heat that washed over her. He seemed to be on fire.

Niall didn't move, but she could have sworn she heard a low hiss escape from between his lips.

Their eyes met in silent question, and when he nodded, she continued her exploration by running her hand down the long length of his arm and over the swell and bulge of muscle, amazed at how hard it was. If he wasn't so warm, it would be like touching a granite wall.

But he was warm—as was she—and getting warmer by the moment. The burgeoning heat made her bold. She gave her hands free rein, exploring not just his arms, but his back, his chest, and then… his stomach.

When she bent over to get a closer look at the bands her fingers were tracing across his stomach, she felt him tense.

She looked up. "Did I hurt you?"

"God, no," he gritted out from between clenched teeth. "It feels incredible. But you are making me hard, and I do not want to frighten you."

She didn't know what he meant at first, but then her gaze dropped down from her fingers, and she saw the enormous bulge between his legs.

Surprisingly, it didn't frighten her. It made her bolder.

She went on playing with the muscles on his stomach and watching them jump with tension under her fingertips.

It took her a few more minutes to realize how tightly Niall was holding himself and what her touch was doing to him. It seemed to be agonizing but pleasurable at the same time.

She looked up into the taut expression and gave him a catlike grin. "I thought you said it wouldn't hurt."

"I lied," he said gruffly. His hot gaze meeting hers. "But this kind of hurt I like."

"I like it, too, but I think…"

"What?"

"I think I should like you to touch me, too."

He gave a deep groan that settled right to her toes. He drew her into his embrace and right before putting his mouth on hers reminded her, "You are in control, Annie. When you tell me to stop, I will."

Annie nodded. But when his mouth touched hers, she wasn't sure she ever wanted him to stop.

For the first time in a long time, in the embrace of the man she'd once loved with her whole heart, Annie MacGregor felt safe.

NIALL TOOK IT SLOW. REALLY SLOW. HE LET HER take the lead even though every part of his body was radiating with pounding blood from her touch.

He didn't think he'd ever been so aroused in his life. Her innocent exploration had been like a lightning rod of pleasure roaring through his veins. He'd had to clench the edge of the wooden stool he was sitting on with his hands so as not to be tempted to reach out and touch her.

But that was nothing compared to the sensations pouring through him now. The feel of her soft lips moving under his was almost too much to take.

God, she was sweet. Like sugar dissolving under his heat. He couldn't get enough, couldn't taste her deep enough to quench the thirst that had been building in him for two long years.

But he didn't put his tongue in her mouth. He waited for her to deepen the kiss. For her to remember. For her to open her mouth and slide her tongue against his.

When she did, he nearly lost his mind. His head exploded. Both of them.

Jesus, this wasn't going to be easy. But he knew that however hard it was—literally—he had to do what it took to make her feel safe.

He had an idea about how to do that and to ensure that he kept his promise not to touch her. Normally, he wasn't into this kind of bed sport, but he had a feeling that with Annie that might change.

As their kissing grew more frantic and her hands started to roam across his chest and stomach again, he knew he had to do something. He started to unbuckle the leather belt at his waist.

When she pulled back suddenly, he realized she'd misinterpreted his actions.

"Don't worry, sweetheart. It's not what you think." He handed the belt to her. "I want you to bind my hands behind my back."

From the way her eyes widened, Niall knew he'd shocked her. But he also knew she understood.

Her face was still flushed from their kiss as she

met his gaze. "This is what you meant about me being in control?"

He nodded. "You can do whatever you want to me, and I won't be able to touch you."

"What if I want you to touch me?"

His cock twitched, and he nearly groaned. "You can unbind me."

She held his gaze for a few more moments, her cheeks growing even more flush. "Is this proper?"

Hell, no. And he probably shouldn't even be suggesting it, but Annie had never been one to let others dictate her mores. "Do you care?"

Her mouth curved with a wickedness that should have concerned him. "No."

She moved away from her position between his legs to secure the belt. Instinctively, he flexed against the bindings and felt the thin strip of leather biting into his wrists.

She'd done a damned fine job—too good a job. He didn't think he could get his hands free if he wanted.

She must have read his mind, because as she came back around, her smile reminded him of a cat that Niall swore would smile when it caught a mouse.

"Now what?"

"You do whatever feels good. Whatever you want."

Her temporary bravado seemed to have deserted her. She bit her lip uncertainly. "I might need some suggestions on where to begin."

Niall wasn't as experienced as she might think—especially on the subject of women pleasuring themselves without his touch—but he had some idea. "You could sit on my lap and straddle me like you might ride a horse."

It took her a moment to figure out what he meant. Her eyes darted to the bulge in his pants, which had calmed a little but got hot fast enough with her eyes on him, and then back to his face. "You can…?"

He couldn't suppress the groan that tore from his chest as the image of her riding him, sliding up and down on his cock faster and faster as she took her pleasure, sprang right to the front of his mind and wouldn't go away. "Yes. There are many different ways to make love, Annie."

And he wanted to show her every one of them.

That seemed to be all the invitation she needed. She lifted her skirts and climbed on top of him carefully so as to not tip the stool, but she needn't have worried. His feet were like steel rods planted solidly in the ground. There was no way in hell he was going to miss this.

He cursed himself for the leather pants that prevented him from feeling her naked against him. But just knowing how little separated their flesh made him hard and throbbing. He groaned again at the sensation, at the feel of her weight on him as she grabbed his shoulders for balance and settled into his lap.

She had no idea how those little movements were driving him half-crazed with lust.

"The leather is cool," she said. "But buttery soft."

As if to prove her point, she innocently moved up and down on him. His arms flexed, instinctively straining at the constraint as another groan tore through him. This one deeper and heavier.

"That feels good," she said, unable to hide her

surprise. She sounded like a bairn who'd just dis-covered a new toy. She met his gaze. "You feel good."

Niall's next groan was smothered by her kiss.

CHAPTER EIGHT

ANNIE HAD NEVER FELT SO wicked and sinful. But neither had she felt so powerful. It was as if she'd just been handed a potent weapon to wield on her own.

No, not on her own. Even with his hands tied behind his back and her setting the rhythm of their lovemaking, Niall surrounded her. Overwhelmed her with his heat and the force of his desire. But it didn't frighten her.

Maybe it was because of his bound hands or maybe it was just because it was Niall, but it didn't matter. Annie felt… desire. Real passion for this man whom she'd once loved with every piece of her heart.

She started slow. Letting the sensations gradually build from inside her, like the soft glow of a candle that is slowly fanned to a flame—and then to a fire. She felt it rising in her like a wave moving closer to the shore.

The feel of his mouth moving over hers, his tongue twining and twisting with hers in a hot, sensual dance…

It was making her weak and fierce at the same

time. Her heart pounded, her breath raced, but her limbs softened. Turned fluid. Her bones dissolved.

She couldn't seem to get close enough. The hands that braced against his shoulders drew around his neck to pull him closer.

Their chests touched.

He growled and she moaned at the sensation of her nipples tightening. Throbbing at the contact.

Contact wasn't enough. She wanted to meld into him. Press and rub.

But it wasn't just her breasts that wanted to feel him. The soft place between her legs started to ache. Started to quiver. Started to crave pressure.

Started to crave hardness.

And Lord, he was hard. The bulge in his pants had seemingly turned to steel. Steel draped in leather.

Her hips started to move with the rhythm of their kiss—of their tongues. She thrust forward and back. Moving over the hardness. Pressing. Rubbing. Grinding harder and harder.

And then her mouth fell away and it was just her hips. Just her moving against him with an insistence that she didn't understand. Something was coming over her. Building. Climbing. Taking her on a path of its own.

Her heart started to pound. Her breath started to hitch. Tiny little sounds of impatience came from between her lips.

And Niall was right there with her. Urging her on with words of encouragement. Words she didn't understand.

"That's it, sweetheart," he whispered in her ear. "Come for me. God, you are so damned beautiful."

Vaguely, she was aware that his voice sounded

strange. Tight and strained. As if he was clenching every muscle in his body.

That's how she felt, too. As if every muscle in her body was clenching and clenching and...

They let go. Her body released in a spasm of pleasure so intense she had to cry out. It radiated through her like an effervescent wave of shimmering light.

Only when the last tingles of pleasure had seeped from her limbs did she realize something else.

The pleasure she thought to never feel again wasn't enough. She wanted more. She wanted Niall to be a part, too.

Tentatively she unfurled herself from where she'd collapsed on top of him and slid her hands around to the waist of his leather trews.

His expression when it met hers was as fierce as it was tender. She could see how moved he was by what had just happened, but also that it had not been done without significant pain to him.

"Tell me what to do," she said huskily, her voice sounding as if she'd just woken after a long winter's nap. "I want to try."

NIALL WAS STRUGGLING TO DO THE RIGHT THING, overwhelmed with the emotion of seeing her bring herself pleasure for the first time as well as overcome by the lust she'd wrought upon his body in doing so.

He wanted nothing more than to take her up on her sweet offer. To tell her how to take him in her hand and slide his cock into the soft, wet place she'd just made for him.

But though her body might be ready for him, her mind might not be, and he couldn't take the risk. Not when her first foray into lovemaking had gone so much better than he'd ever expected.

The belt had been a real inspiration. Although his arms were starting to ache a little.

He had to remind himself that this was not a race. But God, did doing the right thing hurt.

With very real regret, he shook his head. "I think that's enough for today. One step at a time."

She frowned in a way that made him think that he wasn't the only one feeling a little sexual frustration. The knowledge that she wanted him played havoc with his good intentions for a moment before he shook them free.

"But what about you?" she asked.

"I'll be fine," he lied. He wasn't quite sure his bollocks would ever return to a normal color after reaching what must be a bright shade of blue.

Clearly, she didn't believe him and moved her hand over him to prove him a liar. Just the feel of her hand covering him was enough to make him tighten against the urge to come.

Jesus, he was close to shaming himself like an untried lad with his first maid.

But maybe that was closer to the truth than he realized. It felt like the first time because in many ways it was. It was the only time that had ever been important.

"Tell me what to do," she repeated, this time with an insistent squeeze.

He wanted to rip her hands away, but the damned belt had left him at her mercy.

He should have known better. Annie wouldn't have any mercy. Not when she wanted something.

"Damn it, Annie. I told you it's not a good idea." He pulled at the belt again. "Untie me."

She sat back on his lap, considering him for a moment. "No." She paused and repeated in a more certain voice. "No, I don't think I shall. Not until you tell me how to bring you pleasure. I assume there is more than one way?"

Niall swore, cursing himself for a fool. This is what happened when you let a lass be in charge. They took over! Although try as he might, he really didn't wish it otherwise in this case.

Just the thought of her hand on him. Milking him. Making him come.

He swore again. "I don't want to scare you."

She met his gaze. "You won't. I'll be in control, right?"

God, yes. He might have said that aloud. Niall's cool head gave up, and the hot one took over.

He told her exactly what to do. How to free his erection from the tight binds of his trews. How to circle him in her hand. How to stroke him. How to make him come. Which, with the sensuous way she was looking at him as she touched him, took an appallingly few strokes before he couldn't hold on any longer.

He surprised them both. She pushed back off his lap as if she'd done something wrong. "Did I…? Are you…?"

A fierce wave of protectiveness made his already-hurt ribs tighten even more. She was so damned innocent. Even after what she'd been through.

The spasms of pleasure that had wracked his body

were just beginning to ebb when he managed to connect his brain to his mouth again to find the words to answer her. "I'm fine, Annie. Better than fine. That was incredible."

The expression on her face as she brought him pleasure wasn't something he would soon forget. He suspected the only thing that would top it would be the expression on her face when he finally made love to her.

Instead of pleasing her, however, his words seemed to bother her. She started to turn away, and he tried to reach out to stop her—forgetting that his hands were still bound. Seeing him struggle, she hesitated a moment. For one long heartbeat, he thought she might leave him like that. But fortunately her gaze fell on the bandage securing his broken ribs, reminding her that he was injured, and she moved around behind him to untie his hands.

The rush of blood that returned to his arms and shoulders as the belt was released was almost painful. It took a minute to shake out the needles and let the feeling return to his hands before he could clean himself up with one of the extra bandages and fasten his trews.

She watched him quietly with a somber expression on her face and only spoke when he reached for his shirt. "I'll do it," she said. "You shouldn't lift your arms."

Niall sat back down on the stool and allowed her to help him pull the shirt over his head and thread his arms through the openings, all the while replaying in his head what had just happened to try to figure out what he'd done wrong.

He swore. He'd gone too fast. He shouldn't have

let her talk him into pleasuring him. He caught her this time, before she could move away. "I'm sorry."

She frowned. "What are you apologizing for?"

"I rushed you, and now you are upset."

She shook her head. "That isn't why I'm upset."

He frowned. "Then I don't understand. What else did I do wrong?"

She looked up at him, clearly frustrated. "You didn't do anything wrong. Don't you see? That's the problem."

Unfortunately, he didn't see at all. The lass was talking in riddles. But as she looked close to tears, he didn't know what to say. "Why is that a problem?"

ANNIE COULD SEE NIALL'S CONFUSION AND KNEW she wasn't making any sense. But how could she explain the feelings inside her causing such turmoil? He didn't understand. He would never understand. How could he?

What had just happened had been incredible—miraculous in so many ways. The passion she'd felt the first time they'd kissed in Dunvegan was nothing to the passion that she'd just experienced. She'd never dreamed that those kinds of feelings could come over her. That her body could be capable of reaching such heights of pleasure after the violence that she'd experienced.

It had been nearly perfect.

But that was the problem. That was what had caused the wave of sadness that had hit her when she realized the pleasure she had brought him—

and the pleasure he'd so selflessly given her. It made the contrast of what had happened to her that much harder to bear.

He took her by the arm and faced her toward him. "Talk to me, sweetheart. Tell me what is bothering you."

"It's just all wrong."

His face fell. He appeared stricken by her words. "I'm sorry if I disappointed you—"

Her frustration ran over, and she stopped him before he could take more blame that didn't belong to him. "Blast it, Niall! You didn't disappoint me."

"Then why are you mad?"

"I'm not mad," she snapped, realizing she sounded ridiculous. She looked at him, the emotions that had been locked up tight finally breaking free. "That isn't true. I *am* mad. I'm mad at the three bastards who raped me. Who took something that should have been special and pleasurable and turned it into something painful and ugly. I'm mad that the first time a man touched me, it was with cruelty and violence and not with love and tenderness. I'm mad because it should have been different." Her eyes met his accusingly. "I'm mad because it should have been with you."

Her words appeared to hit Niall hard. He looked stricken, as if she'd finally managed to get her blade into his gut.

"I'm sorry, Annie. Sorrier than you will ever know. It's my fault. If I hadn't been such an idiot, none of this would have happened."

Annie felt something inside her jar—like a note played out of tune. Is that what she thought? Had she secretly blamed Niall for what had happened to her?

She feared that maybe she had.

But hearing him say the words made her realize how wrong they were. What happened to her had nothing to do with Niall. Even if they'd been engaged or married, it wouldn't have changed anything. Colin Campbell's men would have hunted her down wherever she was, and Niall wouldn't have been able to protect her from betrayal any more than her brothers had.

The only people to blame for what had happened to her were Colin Campbell and the three Campbell soldiers who'd raped her. She felt a few more cracks opening in the shield that she'd erected around her heart as resentment she didn't realize she'd been harboring fell away.

"What happened to me had nothing to do with you," she said, meaning it. "Even if you had asked me to marry you at Dunvegan, it wouldn't have changed anything."

"You would have been my wife. I could have protected you," he said staunchly.

"Better than my brothers?" Niall's mouth pressed in a hard line. It was clear he wanted to say "yes," but equally clear that he knew it would be wrong. "That is why learning to defend myself is so important to me. The men in my life will not always be around to fight my battles for me." Something suddenly occurred to her. "Why were you fighting with the Campbells earlier? Alys said she saw you throw Connell Campbell across the table." She made a face. "I have to admit, I'm not sorry. I don't much like the way he looks at—"

Me.

She stopped with a gasp, turning to him with a sudden glint of understanding. "The fight was about me, wasn't it?"

"It had nothing to do with you," Niall said, his expression far too blank.

"You're a horrible liar. He must have said something. I thought you promised to stop being my personal avenger?"

Niall didn't say anything, but his jaw clenched a little.

"What did he say?"

"Nothing." Then realizing she wasn't going to believe him, he amended, "It's not important."

"Obviously it was important enough for you to throw him across the table in the middle of the feast." Annie tried to stare him down, but she knew from the stubborn set of his jaw that she wasn't going to pry it out of him. It must have been bad. "It doesn't matter," she said finally. "I can guess the gist. I am either a whore or forever unclean after what those men did to me."

There was more than a faint note of bitterness in her voice as she started to turn away.

"Don't talk like that," he said, stopping her. "It isn't true."

"Isn't it?" she demanded, staring into the hard, blue-eyed gaze of the man who thought he could take on the world for her. "Tell me then why I'm either looked at as a figure to be pitied or scorned—as if I must have done something wrong to encourage those men in their vile deed. Will you fight everyone who gossips or says something nasty about me?"

He gave her a fierce look. "If I have to, damn it."

He was serious. To a proud man like Niall, he would never be able to stand by and let the smirks and whispers that she ignored go unanswered. He would consider it his duty to right every slight, to demand retribution—whether she wanted it or not. Just as he'd done with Colin Campbell.

The futility of it would only make them both miserable. The spark of hope she'd felt a few moments before dimmed.

"Annie, I want you to come with me—"

The sound of the door slamming against the wall as it was thrown open cut off whatever Niall was about to say. Two men barged into the small room but came to an abrupt stop when they saw Niall and Annie alone. But it was worse than that. Niall and Annie looked as if they'd just been doing exactly what they *had* been doing.

Instinctively, Niall moved around to stand in front of her, as if he could protect her from what was about to come. But it was too late. The knowing look that passed between the two Campbell soldiers said enough.

"Sorry to interrupt," the first man said. It was hard to see his mouth behind the heavy dark beard, but Annie suspected it was curled in a smirk. "We were looking for the healer."

Both men had obviously been in the brawl earlier. The second man was holding a blood-soaked cloth up to his face that explained their purpose.

Though there was nothing overtly suggestive in the soldier's voice, it was clear the men had guessed what they'd very nearly interrupted.

Annie's cheeks flamed with mortified heat, realizing exactly what the men would have seen had they walked in a few minutes earlier. Unfortunately, her blush did not go unnoticed and only served to confirm their suspicions.

"She was just here a minute ago," Niall said, trying to salvage Annie's already-ruined reputation. She should have told him not to bother. Now at least there would be reason for the gossip. But she would not—could not—regret it. Even if they had no future together. "The healer went to fetch something. I'm sure she'll be right back."

"I'm sure," the first man said, sounding anything but.

Niall turned to her. "Wait for me outside, and I will escort you back to your room."

Annie guessed what Niall was going to do, but no amount of "persuasion" on Niall's part would stop the inevitable flow of gossip from these two. Knowing he would try anyway, she shook her head. "That isn't necessary." Embarrassment forgotten, she turned to the two Campbells with a smile. "We were finished anyway."

Niall frowned at her word choice, which seemed to confirm the soldiers' suspicions, as the two Campbells did their best to smother their snickers. But she wasn't going to bow her head and slither away in shame. Not anymore. She was a MacGregor, and it was time she remembered it.

Let them gossip. Let them say what they wanted about her. It didn't matter. She knew the truth. She had done nothing for which she should be ashamed.

She would not hide away any longer. It was time for Annie MacGregor to put what had happened behind her. All of it. For good.

CHAPTER NINE

WHAT THE HELL WAS THAT about? Niall didn't have time to ponder Annie's strange behavior. Did she want everyone in the castle to know what they'd been doing?

He would have gone after her, but not five minutes after leaving the two Campbells in the infirmary with very detailed and gory threats of what would happen to them if Niall heard a word about finding him and Annie together, one of Niall's men tracked him down as he was making his way across the *barmkin*.

A short while later—just long enough to change into his armor and gather his weapons—Niall was riding out the gate, hell bent for leather. Or rather, bent for hell. For that was where his prey would soon be headed.

He didn't tell Annie where he was going. He knew she would be furious and try to stop him, and he didn't want to lie to her. Promise or not, this was something he had to do.

❧

ANNIE REFUSED TO LET THEM SEE HER PAIN—OR her humiliation. Just when she was beginning to forgive him, Niall deserted her without a word.

And it didn't escape the notice of anyone.

She'd come downstairs the morning after their interlude in the infirmary, expecting to see him, and had been unable to hide her shock to learn that he'd left the day before. Her brother and sister-in-law had seen her reaction, and Annie didn't know what was worse: Patrick's fury and threats to kill the bastard for hurting her again or Lizzie's heartfelt sympathy.

Annie's vow not to be the object of pity or scorn anymore had taken a drudging. Each day that she entered the hall, it was harder and harder to hold her head high and her shoulders square under the onslaught of stares and whispers—some kind, some cruel.

"What did she expect… that he would marry her?"

"Of course he left. He got what he wanted, didn't he?"

"Poor lass, no one will ever want her after what happened to her."

"It's no more than she deserves, carrying on like that— what man wants a woman who dresses like a man and tries to learn warfare? It isn't natural."

She couldn't believe that after what they'd shared in the infirmary, he would just leave her like that. He'd helped her find her passion again. Something that she'd thought irretrievably lost. But Alys had been right. In time, with the right man, Annie would heal.

There had to be an explanation. But why would

Niall leave without a word?

Finally, after eight days, Annie couldn't stand the stares anymore. She had to get away. Escaping the stifling confines of the castle, she made her way down to the banks of the loch under the watchful gaze of her brother's guardsmen who were patrolling the battlement. She'd brought a pole for fishing and found a quiet spot near the bank to sit on a rock while waiting for her line to jump.

But it was she who jumped a short while later at the sound of a familiar voice. "You shouldn't be out here alone, although you did save me from trying to figure out how to sneak into the castle tonight."

Niall!

Telling her foolish heart to get back into her chest and stop beating so desperately, she looked to her left in the direction she'd heard his voice but didn't see him.

"Don't turn around," he said. "It's better if no one knows I'm here."

Recalling the hurt of his sudden abandonment, she said stiffly, "Why are you here? I thought you'd gone."

She heard a sound of movement and, despite his warning, turned. She gasped as she saw him step out from behind a tree. He looked horrible—as if he hadn't bathed or slept in days. His face was streaked with dirt and grime, his jaw was covered in a grizzled, week-old beard, his eyes were bloodshot, and his plaid and leather *cotun* were splattered and caked with mud as if he'd been riding hard for hours.

He frowned at her question—and her tone. "I'm here for you. I'm sorry I had to leave so suddenly, but it couldn't be avoided."

That was all the explanation she got for his disheveled appearance after eight horrid days of believing he'd deserted her? All those conflicted feelings she'd been wrestling with sharpened into one: anger.

"Where did you go that was so important?" she demanded.

"It doesn't matter."

"Obviously it did for you to leave like that and return looking as if you'd just been dragged through the mud for days."

"I'll explain later, but I don't have much time. I'm here for you. I want you to come with me to Ireland."

She looked at him as if he'd just said he wanted to take her to the moon.

"Ireland? What are you talking about?"

"I can't stay here. Suffice it to say that as an out-law my prospects are slim. And a fresh start could be just what you need as well."

What had brought about this sudden urge to flee? She didn't care what other people thought, but did it bother Niall? The suspicion niggled at her. "Is this about what happened at the feast?"

It took him a moment to realize she meant the men who'd interrupted them in the infirmary. "No, of course not. But surely you can see the benefit of a fresh start? Of going to a place where our pasts will not follow us."

Her eyes narrowed. "You mean where people don't know I was raped."

He appeared taken aback by her bluntness. But she wasn't going to ignore it, and neither was he.

Not if there was any hope for them. Was there any hope for them? Not if he couldn't find a way to deal with the gossip and the unkind things that were said about her. Running away wasn't any more of a solution than acting as her personal avenger.

"It might make things easier for you."

And he wouldn't have to hear the unpleasant things people said of her. God, after all this time, nothing had changed, had it? First, he didn't want to marry her because she was a MacGregor, and now he didn't want to marry her unless they moved to a different country.

You don't think I'm good enough for you.

Annie felt a fresh slap of hurt as her previously spoken words echoed in her head. Dunvegan might have been two years ago, but the wound he'd inflicted had not yet fully healed.

"And easier for you," she said quietly. "You won't have to listen to the unpleasant things people say about me."

He frowned. "That has nothing to do with it. I don't care what people say. But I can't stay here, and I want you to go with me. I want you to marry me."

"And live in Ireland," she finished. "Where we don't know anyone."

And no one knows I was raped.

She wanted to quiet the voice, but the timing was hard to ignore. First the gossip that had sparked the fight in the hall, then those men discovering them alone, and now this?

Maybe she shouldn't be so suspicious of his motives. Part of her wanted to believe him—the determined man before her was no longer the feckless youth who didn't know what he wanted— but the other part couldn't forget standing in that sunny *barmkin* of Dunvegan and being told that he couldn't marry her because she wasn't good enough. Or his shame when she'd challenged him with the truth.

"I do have some connections. Ireland is where I went after the raid. There is some land in Ulster in the district of Glenconkeyne that was once held by the Lamonts. Years ago, during the time of the Bruce, the two lines of Lamonts ended up on different sides of the war. My ancestor, Ewen Lamont, Chief of the Lamonts of Ascog, sided with the Bruce, but the Toward chief sided with the Comyns, and eventually that branch of the clan was driven out of Scotland. They settled in our ancient homeland of Ireland." Annie knew that the Lamonts claimed descent from an O'Neill prince of Ulster. "The Toward chief reconciled with the crown later, and the clan returned to Scotland, but some of my kinsmen stayed on in Ireland as vassals of our kinsman the O'Neill, Earl of Tyrone."

Annie didn't know much about Irish politics, but everyone had heard of the recent "Flight of the Earls." "Didn't the current earl just flee to Spain?"

Niall nodded. "One of his vassals, Donal O'Cahan, has claimed the former Lamont lands, but my kinsman has told me they are mine if I can take them." He smiled. "It's tough, rugged country, and I won't lie. There will be challenges, and we will have to live simply for a while, but I promise it will be worth it."

"And naturally you assumed I would have no

objection to rustic conditions as that is what I'm used to."

Dirty, foul MacGregors. Descended from kings but now little better than peasants.

The taunts that she usually ignored reared their ugly head.

His frown deepened. "I didn't assume anything. I hoped you would want to come with me. I hoped that you would love and believe in me enough to weather the short-term challenges for long-term happiness. I know you are strong and thought you would relish the adventure."

Annie couldn't completely ignore the pang in her heart. It didn't sound so horrible when he put it like that.

Perhaps he sensed her wavering and gave her a smile that could melt her knees and the defensive shield she'd been holding out in front of her. The shield that prevented anyone from hurting her like he had again.

"Ascog Castle was built by my ancestor Ewen Lamont after the war as a testament to his love for his wife and mother," Niall explained. "I will build you an even grander castle when I am done." He took a step toward her. "Don't you see what a great opportunity this can be for us? We can build something together—a home and a future. Something we can be proud of. Not because of who we are but because of what we accomplish."

Despite her lingering hurt and suspicion, the idea resonated. Clearly Niall hadn't lost any of the ambition that had separated them two years ago. Annie knew that as a second son Niall had felt the pressure to make something of himself. Maybe she shouldn't have been surprised at Dunvegan that he'd thought the way to do so was through marriage. But now he'd shifted focus, and all that determination was fixed on Ireland. *Ireland* of all places!

But even if she could be sure his motivation for leaving had nothing to do with her, could she just pick up and leave her home and family? Patrick, Iain and Lizzie were all the family she had left. And despite the years of persecution, she was a Mac-Gregor. She was a part of this land. Of this *Scot* land. She belonged roaming the heather-covered hills and moors of the Highlands.

His head jerked as if he'd heard something. Annie followed the direction of his gaze but didn't see anything.

Still, she felt the urgency in the air. "What is it, Niall? What is really going on? Why the sudden rush?" Her eyes narrowed with suspicion. "What did you do?"

NIALL COULD FEEL HIS HUNTERS CLOSING IN. He knew he didn't have much time. It had been a risk coming here. But a risk he'd had to take.

Maybe he should have confided in her earlier about his plans. But he'd thought they'd have more time.

His time, however, had run out.

He wanted to tell her the reason for the urgency, but he didn't have time to explain. Or rather, he didn't have time for her to get over her anger.

Assuming she got over it, which was probably

a big assumption when it came to this stubborn lass that he loved. But he would never apologize for trying to protect her. Not when he'd failed so miserably before.

That blasted promise! He regretted breaking his word, but she'd backed him into a damned corner.

"You know who is chasing me. Campbells. The king's men. Does it matter? I'm an outlaw. I can't stay here forever."

Her eyes fixed on him like two pointed needles, as if they could prick through his vague explanation. Clearly, she knew he was hiding something.

"I'm not asking you to stay forever," she said. "But you are asking me to leave my home and family for the wilds of Ireland to face war and strife. Surely I deserve more than a few minutes to decide."

"I don't have more than a few minutes." He didn't even have that. "Ireland is not so far away that you cannot come back to visit. And is there any less war and strife here? Patrick may have found peace with the Campbells, but do you think the king is done in his persecution of the MacGregors? What is really holding you here?"

Niall heard another sound in the distance—the precariously *close* distance—and looked east in the direction from whence he'd ridden. He could practically feel the air reverberating with the thunder of hooves hitting the ground. Did he imagine the plumes of dust in the air just beyond the hillside?

He had to go. He couldn't stay any longer. It might already be too late for him to slip through their noose.

He held out his hand to her, begging her to take it. To give him her heart again. He swore he would treat it with all the tenderness and respect it deserved this time. "You have to decide, Annie. I wish I could give you more time, but it has to be now. Are we going to work this out? Will you forgive me for disappointing you and not protecting you or not?"

Annie's eyes grew wide and slightly panicked. She seemed to realize that the time had come but was warring with herself. "I don't know." She looked anxiously back and forth to the castle as if it could provide the answer.

Niall knew it wasn't fair to give her an ultimatum like this, but maybe that's what she needed. They couldn't go on like this forever. If what had happened between them the past few weeks, culminating in the infirmary, wasn't enough for her, what would be? This beautiful woman who'd been hurt in the worst way a woman could be hurt had trusted him. She'd found her passion again with him. That meant something.

"You do know," he said. "You either love me or you don't."

You either forgive me for what happened, or you don't.

"It's not that simple," she protested, clearly anxious. Her hands looked as if she was wringing laundry.

Niall could see in her expression what was going to happen. His hand fell back to his side; the disappointment cutting like a knife. "Actually, it is that simple. What do you want, Annie?"

She looked up at him anxiously. "I…" She took a step toward him. "Niall, I don't…"

The sound of a man's voice stopped her. Her movement had alerted the guards watching her.

"Who is there? Make yourself known. My lady, are you all right?"

"It's all right," Niall said. "You don't need to say anything. I understand."

The problem was that he did. He wanted her to believe in him, but why should she? He'd let her down. He wouldn't believe in him either.

With one last look that would have to hold him for a lifetime, Niall turned and slipped back into the forest.

CHAPTER TEN

THE ANXIOUSNESS THAT ANNIE FELT when Niall demanded her answer was nothing to the panic that gripped her heart as he disappeared into the forest. One minute he was there, and she was debating with herself with what to do, and the next, he was gone as if he'd never been there at all.

The sun dimmed.

The shadows darkened.

The air chilled.

At least it seemed that way. But when she looked up, the sun was still bright and high in the sky. She knew what her mind was trying to tell her. This wasn't what she wanted. She didn't want him to go.

She wanted to call him back, but it was too late. Niall was gone, and her brother's men were already surrounding her.

"I'm fine," she insisted, trying to quell their obvious alarm. "I thought I saw a kitten in a tree."

"A kitten, my lady?" one of the guardsmen asked, clearly confused. "Magnus here said he saw a man."

Annie shook her head, but her attention wasn't on the guardsmen. She was already trying to come up with a plan to rectify her mistake. But she'd have to hurry. She needed to catch up with Niall before he made it to the coast. He'd make for Greenock most likely. It was the biggest port on the Clyde that would have plenty of ships to Ireland. But she'd take one of her brother's best trackers just in case.

The guardsmen were still questioning her as Annie started back to the castle. She would gather a few things and try to convince Patrick—

She stopped suddenly and muttered a curse. Convince Patrick? That would take forever. She would gather a few things and find *Lizzie*. Her sister-in-law would make her brother see sense much faster than Annie could.

She smiled, realizing it was nice to have an ally against her stubborn brother. Patrick wouldn't be too keen to have her go to Ireland, let alone chase after the man who would take her away. Annie could almost hear him yelling about "how dangerous" it was, and that "no sister of his" was going anywhere with "cateran and outlaws about."

Yes, Annie thought to herself, she definitely needed to find Lizzie first.

Now that Annie had made up her mind about what she wanted, she wondered how she could have hesitated even for a moment. She loved Niall, and Alys was right: that was all that mattered. Annie would not let what those men had done take her chance at happiness from her. She wasn't going to hold what had happened at Dunvegan against him forever. Her heart and pride had taken a beating that day, but she would not allow past pain to prevent her future happiness. Whatever additional problems she and Niall had, they could be worked out. He would have to promise not to try to avenge every slight, and she would have to try to forgive his inevitable overprotectiveness. Perhaps Lizzie could give her some help with that as well?

It turned out she didn't need to go in search of her sister-in-law. Annie had just passed through the castle gates when she saw her brother and Lizzie rushing out of the great hall toward her.

"What's the matter?" Patrick demanded, obviously concerned. "We heard the commotion and Donnan said there was a problem outside."

"There wasn't a problem," Annie said.

"My laird," one of the men patrolling the battlements shouted down at Patrick. "There are riders approaching fast." He looked again. "From the banner, it looks to be my lady's brother."

"Jamie?" Lizzie asked. "What is he doing here?"

Annie felt the dread of knowledge slam through her. Dear God. The Enforcer was chasing Niall? What had he done this time?

Her heart sank, guessing exactly what he'd done.

Niall had broken his promise. He'd sworn he would not go after the men who'd hurt her, but he'd done exactly that. Annie had heard Jamie Campbell railing about it for the past half hour.

"When I catch up with him…!" The threat didn't need to be verbalized to be understood. Jamie Campbell was one of the most feared men in the Highlands. The reputation of Argyll's "Enforcer" for ruthlessness was well-known. If he wanted to tear Niall apart "limb-by-limb," he could do it. "Doesn't that damned fool know what I've done for him? The risk I've taken? It's my arse on the line as well this time."

The Enforcer's beautiful wife responded to what was not really a question. Annie had been stunned to see Niall's sister, Caitrina, riding in beside her new husband. But maybe Annie shouldn't have been. If anyone could stand up to Jamie Campbell and not be intimidated by his anger, it was Caitrina Lamont, whose reputation for getting her way was well-known. Niall's once-cosseted and perhaps a little spoiled sister had changed after the horrible destruction of her clan by Colin Campbell. If anyone had wanted his death as much as Annie, it was Catrina. Yet she'd married his brother.

Annie could have sworn she'd seen Caitrina roll her eyes as one of the most feared men in the Highlands went on with his threats. "That 'damned fool' is my brother," she reminded her husband, the blue eyes that so resembled Niall's flashing just as dangerously as the Enforcer's. "And of course, he knows what you've done for him, and the risk you've taken in taking surety for him to Argyll and King James. But you know every bit as well as I do that you would have done exactly the same thing in his shoes."

Jamie's jaw clenched ominously as his gaze fixed on his defiant—and seemingly unconcerned—wife. Perhaps Lizzie hadn't been exaggerating, Annie thought. Had it really been a love match between the brother of the man responsible for her clan's destruction, and Niall's sister? It seemed so.

"That isn't the point," Jamie said to his wife.

"But do you deny it?" Caitrina asked.

"Of course not. Any man who harmed you would soon have his head decorating my castle gate."

"So there," Caitrina said, clearly unbothered by the gruesome threat. "We are in agreement."

"We are in agreement about nothing," Jamie said with a slam of his fist on the table that rattled everyone but his wife. Although actually Lizzie didn't appear to be concerned by the blustery male anger either.

Interesting.

"You will not talk circles around me this time, wife. What I would do is immaterial."

"Is it?" Caitrina asked with a delicate arch of a perfectly formed eyebrow. "I don't think it is at all. How can you fault him for doing exactly what you would have done?"

"Because he lied to me, damn it. He gave me his word he was done killing Campbells."

Niall had done the same to her. But her initial hurt had waned a little during Jamie Campbell's extended tirade.

"Even ones who deserve to die?"

Annie didn't realize she'd spoken aloud until all eyes turned to her. As angry as she was at Niall for breaking his promise—and she was furious— one thing was not at issue: the men who raped her deserved to die. They would argue about whose hand should have wielded the blade later.

No wonder Niall hadn't wanted to tell her where he was going—he knew she'd be furious at his broken promise. Niall's men had hunted down the second man who'd attacked her. According to Jamie Campbell the first had been killed a few weeks ago. Argyll had been furious after agreeing to look the other way with Colin Campbell, and he was demanding that Jamie bring in "the outlaw."

Unfortunately, since then the situation had only gotten worse. The king was now involved. It was his men sent from England who were hunting Niall now, and according to Jamie, after Niall's latest bout of "Highland justice," they were out for blood.

Her personal avenger had been busy—and not very forthright. But at least she could be sure of one thing: his motives in leaving hadn't been based on embarrassment or shame about her. They'd been based on exigency. Any suspicions or lingering questions that she had were gone. The boy she'd fallen in love with had disappointed her, but she knew the man he'd become would not.

"You are upsetting my sister," Patrick said. "If you don't want my blade at your throat, you'll stop."

"You could try. Again, I might point out," Jamie said with a sneer that promised violence.

"Good God," Lizzie said, tossing up her hand with frustration. "Will you two ever stop threatening to kill each other?"

"No," both Jamie and Patrick said at the same time.

"You are both ridiculous," Lizzie said. "Not all problems can be solved with swords."

"This one can," Patrick said under his breath, which was followed by a loud "ow!" when Lizzie's slipper apparently slammed into his leg under the table.

"Your sister is right," Caitrina said to her husband.

"You will not solve this problem with violence, so you better think of another way."

"I don't want to think of another way," Jamie Campbell said flatly—almost belligerently—staring down his wife as if daring her to defy him.

Annie wasn't sure she would have been able to sit still under a stare that withering, but Caitrina appeared bored. At one point, she picked up her hand and studied the back of her nails. She might have been a lioness sharpening her claws in anticipation of the damage she was about to instill on her husband's intentions. "But you will," she said after a few moments with a knowing smile.

The battle of wills continued in a silent stare, and when it was done, it was the ruthless Enforcer who let out a not-so-muttered curse and turned away.

Patrick tried—not very hard—to cover his smirk at his brother-by-marriage, but Annie knew that expression wasn't going to last long. Not with what Annie had to say.

She was right. By the time she was finished presenting her solution, it was Patrick's turn to be furious.

"No! I won't hear of it. You aren't moving to Ireland. What the hell is he thinking to take you into that kind of environment? It's dangerous there!"

"It's dangerous here," Annie reminded him.

"But you have me to—"

He stopped when he saw her expression, remembering what she'd said about protection. Instinct was powerful, and she knew Patrick—and Niall for that matter—would always attempt to protect her. But with time and more practice, she hoped to convince them that her protection wasn't just up to them.

Not that she and Niall wouldn't exchange words on the matter. *Plenty* of words, and some that were likely to be not very ladylike. She'd learned more than hitting a target with the knife from observing the squires.

"You and Lizzie and Iain are the only family I have left," Patrick said, trying a different tack. "I don't want to lose you."

"You won't lose me," Annie said. "Ireland isn't the other side of the world."

"It might as well be," Patrick said with as much belligerence as his brother-in-law had exhibited a few moments before.

"You can't expect Annie to stay with us at Edinample forever," Lizzie interjected with a hand on Patrick's arm that seemed to deflate his anger. "She has to live her own life."

"I don't want to lose my brother any more than you want to lose your sister," Caitrina added gently. "But what Annie says is true. Niall cannot stay here after what he's done, and Ireland is as good a solution as any. Perhaps Argyll and the king's men can be appeased by his exile—at your insistence, of course."

She said the last to her stewing husband, who was obviously still furious at being deprived of his prey. "We'll see."

She leaned over and kissed him on the cheek. "I have all the confidence in you in the world."

He didn't say anything, but Annie could see the flicker of a smile hover around Jamie Campbell's mouth. And his eyes when they fell on his wife were filled with something that could only be called tenderness.

For a moment Annie felt a pang of envy at what Niall's sister had found—even if it was with a Campbell. If they didn't hurry up and agree to escort her to the coast, she was going to lose her chance to have the same.

"Are you sure you want to do this, Annie?" Patrick said.

She felt the weight of all eyes at the table upon her. She didn't hesitate this time. She nodded. "I've never been more certain of anything in my life."

NIALL WASN'T AT GREENOCK. NOR WAS HE AT Dumbarton, Dunoon, or any of the other ports around the River Clyde or the Firth.

With each stop, Annie's panic rose—no matter what assurances Jamie Campbell and her brother gave her. Not surprisingly, Patrick had insisted on accompanying them—and on bringing his own men. The reluctant brothers-in-law worked surprisingly well together, and Annie wondered whether the occasional argument was more out of habit than out of any real animosity. Clearly, there was mutual respect between the two men even if they didn't want the other to see it.

"Don't worry, lass," Jamie Campbell said with surprising kindness after their latest disappointment at Dunoon as they walked back to the place where they'd left their horses. They'd talked to every captain at the pier, but no one had seen him. "He might have gone farther south to avoid Campbell strongholds."

"But they are *your* strongholds," Annie said. "And your brother Duncan's. Niall would feel safer here because of that. No matter how angry you are with him, he knows you won't betray him."

"I wouldn't be so sure of that," Jamie said.

But oddly she was. "He knows this area like the back of his hand, as it's so close to Ascog Castle on Bute. Are you certain he did not go there to say goodbye to his brother and sister first?"

Jamie shook his head. "Caitrina would have let us know by now." Jamie had sent his wife home with a large contingent of men who'd caught up with them a few hours ago. They'd been hunting Niall for almost two days now. "He is probably biding his time in the forest, watching the channel for a smuggling vessel. He'll want to travel at night to avoid questions, and the salt smugglers from Ireland are active in this area."

With the high taxes imposed on the salt that was needed to preserve meat and fish for the long Scottish winters, it wasn't surprising that smugglers from Carrickfergus had taken advantage. Scotsmen considered avoiding the excise man a God-given right and duty.

"I hope you are right," Annie said.

"He is," Patrick assured her. "Eoin tracked him in this direction, didn't he?"

Although Patrick's best tracker had lost Niall's tracks near Ben Lomond, he'd been headed toward this part of the western coastline.

"But what if we missed him?" Annie said, voicing the fear that she'd been trying to keep at bay.

"Then we'll follow him to Ireland," Patrick said fiercely. "If that's what you want."

Relief and emotion gripped her throat. She had to blink back tears as she looked up at her big brother. "You would do that for me?"

"If he will make you smile again, there isn't any place I wouldn't take you."

Annie didn't know what to say. The lump in her throat would take a long time to dissipate.

"What about England?" Jamie said with mock seriousness. "Would you take her to England?"

"Except for England," Patrick qualified quickly. "There are some hells I would not subject you to no matter what the cost."

Annie laughed, grateful for the moment of lightness in what had been a stressful few days on the road.

She eyed Jamie Campbell. There was more to the Enforcer than she'd realized. Good Lord, were there actually two Campbells that she liked now? For a MacGregor, that was worse than heresy.

"We can stay the night at the castle," Jamie said, referring to the royal castle of Dunoon, of which the Campbells were the historical keepers. "My brother Duncan and his wife, Jeannie, are at Castle Campbell, but the servants will be able to ready the rooms and prepare something for us to eat."

Annie wasn't the only one who shuddered at the idea of staying at the Campbell stronghold. "Don't bother on our accounts," Patrick said quickly. "Annie and I will be fine in the village. I haven't recovered from the last time I enjoyed your hospitality."

Jamie Campbell actually grinned. It shocked the breath out of Annie. Maybe she could see what Caitrina saw in him after all. Good gracious, he was a handsome man. A *very* handsome man. It was normally hard to see behind all that *imposing*.

"It was a jest," Jamie said. "I didn't leave you in there for long. And you deserved it. You made Lizzie sad."

Patrick sighed, clearly agreeing. "I'd like to see you in that pit prison for five hours. As a joke, of course. I'd wager you've made your wife sad a time or two."

Jamie chuckled, and Annie had her second shock in as many minutes. The Enforcer laughed? His enemies—mostly MacGregors—would never believe it.

"Maybe once or twice." Jamie admitted, but then he looked to Annie. "Remind me to stay away from Lamont's castle when he gets it built—especially if it has a pit prison."

It seemed she wasn't the only one who was confident in Niall's abilities.

Jamie and his men gathered their horses and rode up the hill that overlooked the port to the castle; Niall, Annie, and their MacGregor clansmen headed to the inn that Jamie had recommended, which was unimaginatively named the Quayside Inn and Alehouse.

While Patrick spoke to the innkeeper about a room and saw to the stabling of the horses, Annie took a seat at a small table in the main room where other travelers were already enjoying the inn's food and ale to wait for him. The room was dark and smoky but warm and relatively clean in appearance, so she did not complain. From the platters going by, the meat pies seemed to be a popular choice. They certainly smelled delicious.

Her stomach rumbled, and she was already mentally preparing her order for when Patrick returned.

Her back was facing the entry, so she didn't see the three men come in. She heard their boisterous laughter, however, as they sat down at a table a few feet in front of her and called for ale.

When she looked up to glance in their direction, she realized one of the men was staring at her. She caught his gaze, and she started with shock. Her heart dropped. Every bone in her body went cold, and her breath seemed to have turned to ice in her lungs.

She would never forget that hideous face. The menacing dark eyes beneath the heavy, even darker brow. The lank black hair that fell across his short forehead as he held her down and forced himself on top of her. The thick neck and shoulders that had seemed like an immovable rock as she'd pressed against him, trying to push him off, clad in the same black leather cotun. The heavy beard that hid most of his face. The brutish features—flat, thick, and pugnacious—like those of a man who did nothing but brawl.

For a moment the fear returned like a drenching, icy shower, rendering her temporarily frozen. She was back in that horrible derelict bothy where they'd taken her to rape her.

But then his mouth drew back in that hideous sneer that she remembered, and her blood started to surge through her veins again.

It started to boil.

He turned to say something to one of his companions, but it was loud enough for her to hear. "I think we found a way to get our reward, lads. We don't need to find the outlaw. He will come to us."

Annie knew exactly what he meant, and it only fueled the firestorm of rage racing through her. She would never let them use her to get Niall.

When they came to get her, she went with them willingly, did not put up a fight, and let them lead her outside. But just as she was about to slip the dagger from the opening she'd made in the folds of her gown, disaster struck.

CHAPTER ELEVEN

❧

AFTER LEAVING ANNIE AT EDINAMPLE, Niall had nearly ridden right into a patrol of the king's men and had been forced to take refuge in the Lomond Hills before rejoining his men—two days later than originally planned—at Balquhidder. The delay had proved a blessing. Not only had it given him time to realize that he had to go back for Annie—and that he would keep going back until she agreed to come with him—his men had also delivered him the location of the third man.

Niall had tracked Callum Campbell to Dunoon— where the soon-to-be-dead man was apparently visiting his sweetheart—and had watched him go inside the inn. Niall would have to wait for him to come out before confronting him. The fewer witnesses the better. But nothing would stop him from finishing this.

Expecting a long wait, Niall had sent most of his men down the street to find some food from another alehouse. He stationed the three men who'd remained around the inn to make sure his prey couldn't escape. Niall had just taken position himself on a stone fence opposite the inn where he could watch the door when it opened.

What he hadn't expected was to see Callum Campbell coming out a few minutes later with a woman. And not just any woman, *Niall's* woman.

The bastard had his arm around Annie's neck and was dragging her out beside him.

Niall saw red. Rage unlike he'd ever experienced before descended over him. His first instinct was to reach for his dirk and throw. But with Annie in the way, it would be too risky.

Instead Niall drew his *claidheamh-mòr* from the baldric at his back and planned the course of attack that would kill the Campbell scourge and his two companions before they had time to react. As the top of Annie's head fell well below the bastard's neck, Niall had a clear path to take off his head. If his blade went through clean, he might be able to kill them all with one swing, using momentum to propel him. At the most, it would take two.

He saw the precise movements play out in his head like a deadly dance. He'd been in this position many times before, although never had the consequences been so dire.

He'd failed Annie once. He would not do so again.

Niall was just about to make his move when one of his men, obviously having seen what was happening, came from around the building to help him. Niall waved him back, but it was too late. Callum Campbell had caught the movement and drew a blade to Annie's throat.

"Whoever is there, step forward or the bitch dies."

As if to prove his words, he pressed the blade into her neck until Annie cried out and a thin seam of blood appeared along the milky white skin of her neck.

Niall growled and lunged forward but stopped cold when Annie cried out again in more pain. The blade was digging deeper, and from the look on the bastard's face, Niall knew he would not hesitate to kill her. The woman who was everything to Niall was nothing to him. Whatever advantage Niall had in skill evaporated into the evening mist. Callum Campbell was in charge, and they both knew it.

"I hear you've been looking for me," the man said with a malicious smile. "Well, you found me. Lucky for me, I found her first." He leaned down and put his nose in Annie's hair, inhaling deeply. "I'd forgotten how good you smelled. I carried that scent with me for days. I'm looking forward to having you again."

Annie made a small sound of terror, and Niall let out a pained sound of frustration, rage, and hatred. His body was teeming, his muscles flexed and rigid with restraint. He felt like a chained lion with its prey just out of reach.

"Let her go." Niall lowered his sword and stepping forward. "Take me instead."

"Niall, no!" Annie cried. "They'll kill you."

Niall ignored her plea, his focus on the man holding her. He couldn't look at her; it would only weaken him more.

"Do we have a deal?" Niall said impatiently. Every second that blade was held to her neck was killing him.

"I'll have to think about it. The bitch might be a MacGregor, but there's nothing wrong with her face... or her body. I still dream of those ripe paps." The bastard had a lecherous gleam in his eye as his hand moved up to cup her breast.

Annie reacted as if burned, trying to wrench out of his hold, but it only caused the knife at her neck to dig in deeper. She made a sound like a wounded animal that made everything inside Niall disintegrate. He'd never felt so damned helpless in his life.

He couldn't fail her again. God wouldn't be so cruel. Agony twisted through him like a hot blade tearing him apart. He had to think of something.

"Niall!"

He forced himself to look at Annie, unable to ignore her plea, but scared at what he might see. Scared at seeing the fear and helplessness reflected back at him.

But that wasn't what he saw at all. Instead he saw hatred that burned as hot as his and cold determination. He saw strength, not vulnerability.

He'd forgotten what she'd learned—what he'd taught her. And all at once, he knew what was going to happen. It was as if in that one look, they'd exchanged thoughts.

The bastard didn't even know what hit him. With quickness and purpose that Niall would praise her for later, Annie found the hilt of the knife he'd given her and moved it straight back into a vulnerable spot in the bastard's groin.

The Campbell moaned in shock and pain, and the knife he held to Annie's neck fell to the ground. Annie pushed away as Niall lifted his sword above his head. When it fell, it took the bastard's life with one clean sweep.

His Campbell companions suffered a similar fate a few moments later when Niall's men rushed forward, the MacGregor battle cry echoing through the air.

But Niall wasn't paying attention. He'd already dropped to the ground to face Annie, who'd fallen to her knees after stabbing the Campbell. She'd known to get out of the way of Niall's sword.

She still held the bloody dagger in her hand and looked up at him with a wide-eyed stunned expression on her face that were it not for the circumstances would have made him smile. "I did it."

Shock slowly turned to pride as the realization of what she'd done sank in. She seemed to grow with confidence right before him. Any fears that she'd be overcome by what had happened or fall apart were put to rest. Annie was a MacGregor. Fight was in her blood. He'd just given her the tools to use it.

"I did it," she repeated. "Just like you taught me. I went right for the vulnerable part of his leg. I didn't know if I could do it, but I did." She looked up at him. "Thank you."

Niall couldn't wait another minute to draw her into his arms. Emotion gripped him hard. He had to fight from squeezing her as hard as his chest was being squeezed. "God, Annie, you have nothing to thank me for. It was all you. I didn't do a damned thing. I never felt so helpless in my life. I thought…" He struggled to find his voice with the tangle of emotions weaving in his throat. "I thought I was going to let you down again."

She smiled. "You didn't let me down. And you

weren't helpless, because you trained me not to be helpless. I wouldn't have been able to do it without you insisting that we repeat everything a hundred times in training. When the time came, I just reacted from experience—I didn't even have to think."

Niall smiled. She was right. Training Annie to protect herself hadn't lessened his ability to protect her—it had enhanced it. "I think it was all the running around the yard that I had you do."

She drew back to look at him and remind him of what was still in her hand by pointing it in his direction. "What did you say?"

Very carefully, he unfurled her fingers from around the hilt—the tightness with which she was still gripping the knife made him think she might be more affected than she realized—and wiped the blade on his pants before handing it back to her to slide it into its sheath. "I said I'm glad all that training paid off, and I'm glad you didn't have to throw the knife at anyone's head." His included. Although, he had to admit, she had exceptional aim. In the future, he'd have to make sure he didn't leave any knives around when they argued. *In the future.* Wait. Did they have a future? As he helped her to her feet, he asked, "What are you doing here, anyway?"

It wasn't Annie who answered, but her brother who came storming around the building with some of Niall's men. "Looking for you, damn it." Patrick took a look at the three bodies piled up in the yard and his face went dark with rage. "What the hell happened?" He turned to Annie. "I left you alone for five minutes!"

Annie shrugged, exchanging a knowing look with Niall before looking back at her brother. "It was an eventful five minutes."

"I'd say," Patrick said dryly. "Damn it, I should have realized that some of Colin Campbell's men could still be around." He looked at the dead men and sighed. "My brother-in-law isn't going to be happy about this."

But Niall wasn't thinking about Jamie Campbell. "Were you really looking for me?" Niall asked Annie, drawing her attention back to him.

Her brother could wait, damn it.

She nodded, for the first time looking a little unsure of herself. "I wanted to tell you that I would like to go to Ireland with you... if you still want me to?"

The relief that rushed over Niall was only overshadowed by his happiness. "Are you jesting? There isn't anything that would make me happier." He pulled her into his arms again, resting his head on hers when she nuzzled into his chest. Nothing had ever felt this good. "Does this mean you forgive me?"

She pulled back a little to give him a chastising smile. "For Dunvegan or for breaking your promise not to go after the men who'd attacked me?"

He winced and smiled a little sheepishly. "Both?"

"I haven't decided yet. But you should have some time to convince me."

"How much time?"

"How does a lifetime sound?"

"Like a damned good start. But I was thinking more an eternity."

And he intended to make every minute count.

He couldn't go back and change what had happened, but he would do his damnedest to make sure that he never gave Annie cause to doubt him again and that the rest of their lives were filled with happiness and love.

Not caring that her brother and his men were watching, Niall couldn't wait any longer to kiss her. He lowered his mouth and covered her lips with his, sealing their promise with all the love and passion in his heart.

It just might take that eternity.

EPILOGUE

Late August 1612, Glenconkeyne, Ulster, Ireland

ANNIE LOOKED DOWN AT THE three disgruntled faces staring up at her with expressions ranging from mulish to straight-out rebellion. They didn't like it any more than she had, but they would learn just as she had that it was for their own good.

"But why can't we have a real knife," Bridget, the eldest of the three girls, protested. "We've been using the stupid old wooden ones for *months*."

The sixteen-year-old said the last word as if it had been years. Annie tried not to smile. It was serious work training these lasses, but good Lord, they made her laugh with their dramatics. Had she been that bad? Suspecting she knew the answer, she bit back a smile. "It's been five weeks, and you still have a long way to go before we practice with real blades. Being a warrior doesn't happen overnight. You have to be patient."

Deidre, the youngest of her three pupils at twelve, scrunched up her nose in a frown. With her blondish red hair, green eyes, and tiny features, she looked like an Irish pixie. A very rebellious Irish pixie. Of the three girls, Deidre was the hardest to keep in line. Her mother said she'd tried to run before she could walk. She also had an uncanny ability to find an opponent's weak spot. "Were *you* patient when you were training?"

Annie sensed the presence that had just come up behind her but did not give any indication that she knew he was there. "I was exceedingly patient. I never gave my instructor any problems and did as he bade all the time."

That instructor made a muffled choking sound behind her, but she didn't turn around. He better not be laughing. Corralling these three was hard enough without Niall undermining her authority—even if she was stretching the truth a hair.

Rose, the fifteen-year-old skeptic in the group, said, "Is that true, my laird? Did the lady go along with everything you said?"

Niall came around to stand beside her. Annie felt the familiar jolt in her heart that never seemed to lessen. If anything, it had only become more powerful since he'd become her husband.

Niall had grown even more handsome in the two years since they'd wed and arrived in Ireland. Her brother and Jamie Campbell had insisted on a "proper" wedding before they'd left. Lizzie and the baby had been sent for, and they'd traveled to Bute to wed at Ascog, where Niall's sister and younger brother lived—before finding a ship to take them to Ireland a few days later.

Just ahead of the king's men.

As Caitrina had foretold, Jamie Campbell had appeased King James by assuring him that "the outlaw" had been "driven" away and would not be causing any more problems in the Highlands.

Jamie hadn't mentioned Ireland, where Niall caused plenty of problems for the next few months while he ousted the king's man and retook the Lamont ancestral lands.

Thanks to Jamie's efforts in the months since, however, Niall had finally been reconciled to the king. He was a loyal subject now. Or as loyal as a subject needed to be in "wild" lands far from the arm of the king's authority.

She and her too-handsome husband exchanged glances, and he read her warning. *Smart man.* Two years of marriage had taught him a few things. She knew how to get her revenge.

Their gazes grew a little hotter as thoughts of just how good that revenge could be filled them both.

"The lady has been an exemplary pupil in all things," Niall said.

Annie caught the reference and hoped the girls attributed the blush in her cheeks to pleasure at the compliment and not the remembered pleasure of something else.

Alys had been right. It had taken time and patience, but as the dark memories faded, Annie's passion had returned full force. They had no need of Niall's belt anymore—much to her wicked husband's chagrin. She trusted Niall completely.

Deidre, however, did not share Annie's trust. She clearly didn't seem to believe him. Nor had she missed his less-than-direct response.

Annie cut her off before the little girl could question him further. "We will resume our practice on Monday." She tried not to smile at the groan of displeasure from her three pupils. To say that Niall had come around on her training was an understatement. And it wasn't because it had only taken her *five* months to hit the target ten times in a row. When Bridgette had been set upon in the woods by ruffians a month ago—and thankfully rescued by her father, one of Niall's men, before the ruffians could harm her—it had been Niall's idea for her to start training the young girls in the area. It had been just what Annie needed. She would never forget what happened to her, but she'd found a way to use it for good. "As I told you, we have important visitors arriving tomorrow."

"I'm afraid there has been a change of plans," Niall interrupted. "Our visitors sent word that they will be arriving in a few hours."

"What!" Annie shrieked. "A few hours? I'm not ready."

Niall gave her a long look up and down, taking in every inch of her tight, formfitting trews (her brother wasn't going to be pleased about that!) and black leather *cotun* that Niall had surprised her with not long after they arrived: "a warrior needs armour—even for practice," he'd told her as she'd blinked back tears. "You look fine to me."

Annie exchanged glances with the girls who shook their heads in shared understanding. Men were so obtuse when it came to such things.

Saying goodbye to the girls, Annie hurried back to the castle with Niall to give the servants their instructions.

They'd only been living in the new castle for a few weeks, but already Conkeyne Castle felt like home. Niall had modeled it on Ascog, the Lamont stronghold that had been razed by Colin Campbell in the raid over four years ago and rebuilt by Jamie and Caitrina. The four-story square tower house and "bawn," as the Irish called the defensive wall surrounding the castle, would have made his ancestor Eoin proud. It had certainly made her proud.

But Annie hadn't anticipated having so many visitors so quickly—and all at once. Patrick, Lizzie, Iain, and her new niece, Mary, were coming, as were Jamie, Caitrina, and their two young daughters, Eliza and Anna, who'd been named in honor of their aunts. Niall's younger brother Brian, whom he'd let become Chief of Lamont in his stead, was also part of the traveling party. It would be the first time they'd seen their family in over two years, and Annie couldn't wait. She also wanted everything to be perfect.

She had never regretted her choice, and she wanted everyone—especially her brother—to see why. She was happy, and they'd built a home here. Something they could both be proud of.

Annie had just finished stepping out of her bath when her husband came into the room. She knew him well enough to know that the timing was not a coincidence.

Niall was ever the opportunist.

"I don't have time," she said, staring at him with water dripping down her back from her still-sopping hair.

He ignored her protest and started stripping off his clothes. There was nothing slow and seductive about his movements. There didn't need to be. Niall Lamont had perfected the seduction of quick and methodical. He disrobed as if there were no other purpose than to take off his clothes. Which made it all the more arousing.

Annie felt her breath quicken and her pulse hitch as inch by inch, muscle by muscle, his powerful naked physique was revealed to her appreciative eyes. The gorging traitors!

But Lord, how she never grew tired of looking at him. The powerful granite wall of his chest. The rock-hard bulges of his arms. The tight ropes that lined his stomach. The firm, perfectly formed backside. The muscular thighs and legs. And the long, thick staff of his manhood that stood proud and prominent, jutting upright against his stomach.

It seemed to be throbbing.

The place between her legs grew a little warm at that. All right, a *lot* warm.

He was beautiful, and that impressive part of him no longer frightened her.

No, she'd grown rather attached to that part of him. *Quite* attached. She liked to wrap her mouth around the heavy hood, slide her tongue down the long vein, and squeeze his bollocks gently in her hand as she milked him with long slow pulls of her mouth.

She nearly groaned as the pleasure pulled with need in that sweet spot between her legs where he liked to lick and flick her with his tongue. She could almost feel him nuzzling. Feel the scratch of his beard between her thighs as he brought her pleasure with his mouth.

Slowly she pulled her mind from the wicked pleasures of their marital bed. She refused to be so easily distracted. "It won't work, Niall."

He cocked a dark eyebrow. "It won't? Hmmm." He let his heated gaze slide down the damp drying cloth that she'd wrapped around herself and fastened on her nipples. Her taut, poking-against-the-linen nipples. "You sure about that? You seem a little tense." He took a step toward her. "How about I help you relax a little?"

She eyed his erection. "Your selflessness is truly astounding."

He grinned. "I didn't say I wouldn't get rid of a little pent-up tension myself." He fisted himself and gave a firm pull, making her envy his hand. She loved to take him in her hand. To feel all that pulsing power in her grip. "It's your fault. You got me all worked up earlier in those trews." He shook his head. "I don't know how I let you talk me into those. They're indecent."

She rolled her eyes. "They are practical. And they are no more indecent for me than they are for you."

He took another step toward her, and she took a corresponding step back. This went on for a few more, until the back of her legs met the bed.

She'd known exactly where they were headed. Why fight it? She'd known where they would end up the moment he'd walked into the room. Her barely clothed body was pressed up against his naked one when she said with a hint of challenge, "What are you going to do?"

"Toss my wife on the bed and have my way with her."

She made a face. "That doesn't sound very fun for your wife."

He grinned—a very slow, very wicked grin. "Oh, I intend to make sure she enjoys it." And then he told her in very detailed, very explicit ways exactly how much fun she was about to have.

By the time he was done, she was pulling him down on the bed on top of her. His mouth was on her lips. Her breasts. The inside of her thighs. And finally…, oh God, it was right there. Nuzzling and tonguing. Flicking and sucking. Making her cry out with pleasure as the first wave of spasms crested over her.

And then he was inside her. Filling her with all that hardness. Thrusting hard and deep. Forcing her to come again and again. Only then did he cry out his own pleasure, long and powerful as he filled her with the warm rush of his seed.

Seed that had already taken root.

But she would hold on to that wee bit of news for another week or two. She wanted to be sure, and her sisters-in-law had warned her that her already overprotective husband would become unbearable when she was with child.

Annie wasn't looking forward to months of sitting on pillows and offering to be carried everywhere, but in the end, when they held their child in their arms, she knew it would be worth it.

But for now, she snuggled deeper into the cocoon of her husband's embrace and savored the moment of peace.

Annie knew that it wouldn't always be like this, but she knew that whatever came their way, they would weather the storm… together.

THE END

ACKNOWLEDGMENTS

Thanks as always to Jami Alden for reading this so quickly and for being the best first reader ever. Thanks also to Kim Killion at The Killion Group, Inc. for the gorgeous cover and print formatting. On the production side, a huge thanks Anne Victory and Linda for their eagle-eyed proofing, and Lisa Rogers for the ebook formatting. I have a great village and couldn't do it without you all—really!

ABOUT THE AUTHOR

Monica McCarty is the *New York Times* and *USA Today* bestselling author of romantic suspense and historical romance. Her books have won and been nominated for numerous awards, including the Romance Writers of America's RITA & Golden Heart, RT Book Reviews Reviewers' Choice, the Bookseller's Best, and Amazon's Best Books of the Year. Known for her "torrid chemistry" and "lush and steamy romance" as well as her "believable historical situations" (*Publishers Weekly*), her books have been translated and published throughout the world. When not trekking across the moors and rocky seascapes of Scotland and England, Monica can be found in Northern California with her husband and two children.

- Visit Monica's website at: MonicaMcCarty. com
- Find Monica on Facebook at: Facebook. com/AuthorMonicaMcCarty
- Follow Monica on Twitter at: Twitter.com/ MonicaMcCarty
- Follow Monica on Instagram at: Instagram. com/MonicaMcCarty
- Sign up for Monica's Newsletter at: Moni- caMcCarty.com/index.php#newsletter

19305821R00117

Printed in Great Britain
by Amazon